Origenesis: Awakening

A Novella by
K.C. Atlas

Copyright Information

This is a work of fiction. Names, characters, places, and incidents either are the product of the author's imagination or are used fictitiously. Any resemblance to actual person, living or dead, events, or locals is entirely coincidental.

Copyright © 2019 by K.C. Atlas

All rights reserved. No part of this book may be reproduced, stored in a retrieval system, or transmitted in any form or by any means, electronic, mechanical, photocopying, recording, or otherwise, without the prior written permission of the author, except as provided by U.S.A. copyright law.

First paperback edition October 2019

ISBN: 978-0-578-59936-6

Self-published by K.C. Atlas
Distribution by Lulu
Lulu.com/spotlight/kc_atlas

Acknowledgements

I began this story when I was in the sixth grade. Every day we had to do a journal entry based on a question on the board in my English class. One day, it happened to be a free-write, and I chose to do a prologue. I really wanted to be in the creative writing class, but the class was full and so I exploited the opportunity to write in this class. Of course, when I had begun this story I did not imagine it would become this long journey, but that day the spark my passion had for writing ignited. My teacher was impressed and had me read it to the whole class. She even sent it to my mom to read, who shared it with my family. Due to this, I had others encouraging my talents, and I would not have finished or even believed in myself if it wasn't for a couple of individuals who always believed in me. These two wonderful women happen to be my mother and her mom, my Meemaw. Without my mom, and my Meemaw, I would have given this story up after the first obstacle I endured. Therefore, I dedicate this story to them. I love you two very much!

Prologue

The bond between brothers is never feeble when twined together, and such was the bond between the young Sacamega brothers, Megahte and Kojax.

Each born with remarkably unique differences, together they triumphed over every obstacle. Megahte, the older one, had a mountainous intellect, and Kojax, the younger by seven years, had a natural dexterity. The two lived together amongst a magical world with enchanting forests, mystical waters, and mythical creatures. Yet their race was condemned to be mundane.

So, with his immense intellect, and Kojax's uncanny dexterity, Megahte strove to unlock the secret of magic, and one fateful day Megahte stumbled across a mysterious stone. He forged a pendant from it and bore it around his nape with an enchanted gold chain. With the ability to harness the forces of magical nature and wield it for himself, he became his world's first wizard.

Kojax, however, grew envious of his brother's newfound skill in sorcery, driven by the hollow need for his presence. He was determined to prove that his natural skill in the art of weaponry was far more superior when enhanced equally.

The twine between the two first then began to unravel, and, coincidentally, so did their world around them. Through devious methods, Kojax simmered his envy by the discovery of Megahte's secret. He, too, forged a pendant, but it was endowed with a silver chain, and, in secrecy, he mastered his own use of the stone. He could not harness the magic he encountered, but could manipulate it after depriving the life from the mythical creature's soul.

One fateful day, the two brothers, incognizant of the path that will later unfold, journeyed to the mysterious ruins of Origenesis , a strange arena on a peninsula off the mountainous

border of the mainland.

What happened next marks the beginning of this story. It was in the center courtyard where Kojax confronted his brother, and this led to the battle that will change the course of history from its roots.

Spitefully, Kojax attacked his elder brother, who was unaware of his brother's newfound skill. Though they fought ferociously, Kojax was the only one to fight mercilessly. He loathed for so long that his love for his brother had dwindled to be nominal. His mind craved bloodlust, and Megahte was soon pinned.

In the final moment, as Kojax lunged forward to end the life of his brother, Megahte reached out and pressed his hand against Kojax's chest as they collided. There was a pause as the two brothers stood together for the last time. Then, after Megahte slipped limply from the grip of his wicked brother, and Kojax's sword unmasked its scarlet colors, thunder echoed above as his tranquil lifeless body struck the ground.

Dark and gloomy clouds filled the air, and, as the drops of rain struck his bloodied sword, Kojax began to wallow in his brother's last act. He became a man enraged and engulfed in the desire to be powerful and to show it to the world. Fueled by this vision, his hate unfurled faster than a rambunctious plague, liberated and eager to blemish all that's known.

Without a moment's notice, he left the Origenesis Ruins and headed back towards the mainland. However, before he reached the mountain pass that separated the peninsula from the inland, the ground began to shake violently. Kojax looked out towards the ocean, and stumbled back in bewilderment.

The sea-level began to plunge rapidly, descending into the desolate unknown. Kojax gawked in confusion but quickly gathered his ground. He turned to seek out an oracle, who he knew could explain the phenomenon. However, the words slivered distastefully in return into Kojax's ear.

"What did you say!" Kojax hissed from within the shade that bathed his body. The anger in his voice boiled evidently.

"It must have happened when you killed your brother," the oracle spoke ever so calmly despite his condition, "but there's a way you can even the odds if you spare me." He smirked half soaked in his chair, his face beaten beyond recognition, as he taunted for Kojax's retaliation.

The oracle had informed Kojax that he was trapped in an alternate reality, a replica of the world he's from, and when the realms realign the prophesied one will extinguish his name and finish the job Megahte couldn't.

Kojax's reign was massive and his motives were vain, so he accepted the oracles wicked offer. The world would soon lay in peril and only the prophesied child could rescue it from Kojax's demented grasp.

Chapter 1

The night lay dormant in tranquility, undisturbed by its many mystical creatures that now lie in slumber. The stars illuminated the incandescent sky, the smell of nocturnal blossoms filled the air, and a cool breeze from the western seas lightly blew through the leaves of the trees.

A small cabin settled peacefully amongst the serene forest, and from within there was a soft orange light that frolicked from the window. Inside, a mother sat over her child tucking him into bed. Her long silk-like hair, cascading like an onyx colored waterfall, tickled the boy's face as she leaned in to kiss his forehead. She smiled at him with eyes like sapphires and whispered a lullaby. Slowly, he drifted into slumber.

-A few hours later-

"Shhh" hushed the women, as she suddenly shook the child. The child's face grew with fear as he woke, and his mouth opened to emit a cry. She covered his mouth and whispered reassuringly, “it's going to be alright.”

She picked him up and carried him to the back of the house. The hollers of men outside echoed rabidly into their eardrums. With teary eyes, she opened a part of the wall that revealed a secret compartment where she placed her child.

"You need to be quiet for mommy, okay?" she demanded; her voice cracked. "Can you do that?" Unable to speak and stricken with fright, he nodded tearfully. She stood with a hand over her mouth to cover her shaken lips and closed the door, restoring the look of a plain wall.

The boy watched his mother through a crevice in the wall, his faced sketched in fear. He wanted to cry, but couldn't, responding obediently to his mother's request. He watched as she picked up a sword that belonged to his father and turned to face the door. Her body trembled as she raised the sword, pointing its extremity straight at the door.

Suddenly the door busted open and a burst of lightning bellowed above, uncovering a shaded figure. It stepped in...--

It was a piercing howl, followed by a loud raucous, that brought Alekos back to reality. Shaken, he took a deep breath before slowly letting it out, as he turned his head up towards the countless sea of diamonds above. His burnt amber eyes shook as tears began to sear the surface of his eyes. He clenched his eyes and jaw before turning towards the noise that roused him.

Below, a dim light flickered and danced behind a shadow that peered from a window. The silhouette drifted out of sight, and soon after, a threshold opened from beneath him. Light flooded across the field, stretching desperately towards the dark, and the shape reemerged.

Within moments, the night silence was broken when a female voice illuminated the serene solitude.

"Alekos, come on inside now."

It was the soft, elegant voice of Caterina, a woman who has cared for him since he could remember. Uneager to end his tranquil and solemn isolation, he sighed and closed his eyes.

“Yes ma'am," he responded.

However, his mind was still set on the memory; it was all just a blur. He sat up, sighing into the refreshing breeze, before edging towards the side of the cottage. The ladder he had used to climb up was still resting peacefully against the side of the roof. Half effortlessly he climbed onto it, provoking an angry creak as the wood strained beneath his weight. It wobbled with each step he took, croaking more so like a frog as he got closer to the ground. He hopped lightly off and turned to face the woman.

Her gaze was set sternly on him, almost as if studying him; it was a constant reminder of her concern. She turned towards the door, revealing her topaz-colored eyes which glimmered in the candlelight.

"I really could have used your help earlier," she said as he came in.

Undeterred, he ignored the comment as he stepped past her into the hut, and immediately retaliated to the beckoning call of his cozy cot. As she turned to blow out the candle on the table, he brushed past her slaying the flame with his gust.

"Now, don't you go to bed with any ill will in you," she snapped, with a stern offended voice, as her glare diverted to him. Alekos turned to face her before carelessly sitting back, bending the bed with his weight.

"You are a good tale, yet your cover is not dignified to show it," she said pitifully, as she reached into a water bucket that trickled refreshingly. When her hand withdrew she held a cloth that melted softly with the water. She clenched it, and the water sifted between her fingers.

"Goodnight Caterina," Alekos murmured as he leaned away from her, but the light by his bed exposed his true colors.

"Is that a cut?" She said as she stepped toward him; her gaze was stuck on the blood that glimmered half dry in Alekos' rough burgundy goatee.

"It's nothing, goodnight," he replied, his voice reservedly expressing his annoyance.

Without reservation, he turned away and pulled back the covers on his bed before turning back to unlace and kick off his boots. Caterina stood there sternly for a while before surrendering, her shoulders resting first as her concern gave in.

"What's wrong?" she questioned as she sat next to him and smiled reassuringly. Alekos looked at her a moment before responding. "I had that nightmare again," Alekos murmured apathetically, “but there was a man this time. I feel like I know him, but his face recalls no memory of mine.”

"Do you think it was your father?" Caterina asked, still worried. Alekos looked over to her before responding.

"No, it couldn't be," Alekos stated. "It felt cold when I saw him. It didn't feel right." He paused and then shook his mind free from reflecting before he looked up to her. "I just need some sleep is all. I'll be fine," Alekos smiled.

Caterina studied him carefully and then nodded in agreement. She stood up and walked across the room to her bedroom. She turned to look at him once more before speaking.

“Goodnight,” she whispered as she closed the door to her room.

Alekos sat pondering as he watched her door until the light around it was consumed by darkness. He grabbed the cloth she left by the bucket and laid back, placing it on his head. Somehow the cold, damp touch of the cloth soothed the unattended wound he received earlier that day chopping wood. He pulled the blanket over him and his mind started to drift. Slowly, he fell asleep.

The next morning when Alekos awoke, he could hear Caterina outside feeding the junglefowl. He kept his eyes closed at first, wanting to savor every ounce of his rejuvenating rest. As he began to open his eyes, he stopped short to rub out the crust that had caked up during the night. He yawned to give some well-needed moisture to his eyes, sat up, and turned to rummage for his boots with his feet. After he fastened them on, the door creaked open, and through the blinding threshold, Caterina appeared smiling with an empty basket in her hands.

“Good morning,” she said as she walked over to the table that separated them, “I had no luck with eggs this morning. Something must have spooked the fowl.”

Alekos peered up at her only for a moment before going back to tucking his breeches behind the folded leather tongue of his boots. “It’s okay. I think I’m going to go to the river,” he responded as he stood up.

After stretching, he strode to the door but stopped as he felt Caterina’s hand reach for his shoulder. He turned, saying nothing, but Caterina didn't seem to want to stop him. She studied his crisp emerald eyes, before letting out a sigh. "If you go into the village, would you mind bringing home something so we don't have to settle with a fowl supper?" Alekos paused but nodded slightly before continuing on his way.

He stepped outside into the bathing sunlight, though the sky was not as welcoming as the temperature. Beyond the trees, Alekos could see the mountains smothered in storm clouds. Thunder could be heard clapping, and lightning illuminated the darkness beneath. Alekos stared momentarily until his attention broke towards the village.

They lived uphill from the community because Caterina craved a more peaceful environment, but Alekos appreciated the tranquility equally. This is why he decided to avoid going through the village to the river by taking the long route. It also saved himself from the adhesive children that follow him everywhere. There was a path in the woods next to their hut that led west through the forest and then north around the village. It was Alekos' personal trail.

Hastily, he made his way towards the trail, the bellowing above being his reminder not to stay out long. When he approached the entrance of his trail a hive of driller bees welcomed him. Though the creatures weren't very hostile Alekos knew to take caution, their massive drill for a stinger spoke for itself.

However, fear triumphed glory in this skirmish, and Alekos carefully went around. Even after he was safely on the trail, their buzz still rang in his ears. Creepy crawlers gave him goosebumps. It was not long though before he made it to the river and was brought back to reality by the sight of what he had come for.

They were beta angels; attractive, colorful fish with a feathery flowing body, yet vicious basilisks under the cover. Secretly carnivorous, they shred and tear all the meat off of anything foolish enough to swim with them.

Alekos enjoyed coming here to watch these masters of disguise. He would sit with his legs hanging over the edge trickling a few feet above the water, and watch as the fish circled beneath him. He knew each one was savoring, in patience, the idea of the feast they saw above them, but he didn't care. He enjoyed the company and felt appreciated when they swarmed anything that disturbed their time together.

After a couple of hours, his tranquility was shattered when smoke was seen reflecting on the surface of the water. Alekos' head swung around as he stood towards the direction of the smoke. It was the village. He broke off towards the smoke, each step propelling him in the direction of the village. He could hear someone yelling, but couldn't make it out beneath his thudding footsteps and heavy breathing.

As he reached the village, he skidded to a standstill. It was the blacksmith; he caught his hut on fire. He was yelling a scene while water jays circled above showering water down below. Alekos arrived just in time to see the peace restored and the order renewed. However, his actions betrayed him when he saw Elrin notice him.

Elrin was the village orphan; after his parents were massacred by beasts in the wild, he clung onto the attention of others.

Alekos was his favorite.

It was too late to turn around, so Alekos knew his solitude was at a definite end for the day. He smiled as Elrin shouted with glee and opened his arms. The boy was very short for being eleven years old, but his style flattered Alekos.

His hair was long and shaggy, like Alekos', but was a brilliant gold color instead of burgundy, and his hair was a mess, unlike Alekos who kept his hair off his face. However, Elrin looked like a mop so he could cover the large birthmark over his right eye. He was self-conscious, but looked up to Alekos and wanted to be just like him.

"Now all you're missing is the beard," Alekos chuckled, as Elrin galloped over to him jumping in his arms. "It won't be long," he replied, his face etched in joy as he gripped Alekos' goatee lightly.

Alekos put him back down and knelt, "I think you got a few more years for that," he chuckled, before changing the subject. "So, are there any special ladies?" Alekos winked, making the boy blush.

"I've seen you around Jada's house a lot, are y'all

friends?" Alekos questioned.

"I'm afraid to talk to her," Elrin admitted, hiding his face beneath his hands.

"To Jada," Alekos giggled, reaching forward to lower Elrin's hands, "a man like you would sweep her off her feet in a heartbeat. What are you afraid of?"

"Judgment," Elrin said as he turned around to face the town and plopped down on Alekos' knee. His gaze turned to Jada, giving away her position.

She was thirteen, and Alekos knew she was a hard catch for Elrin. "You know I have a birthmark too, and no one thinks any differently of me. I'll tell you what," Alekos said, waiting for Elrin to turn and look at him, "You go over there and introduce yourself, and that only, and I'll get you something from the market." Elrin's eyes lit up when Alekos' words hit his ears. He knew what Alekos meant.

"I'll be back," the boy smiled in response as he hopped off Alekos and walked proudly in Jada's direction.

Alekos stood and watched as Elrin made his way to her, but as she looked towards his direction, Elrin quickly spun around. Alekos chuckled and walked over to Elrin, who was now kicking rocks.

"Did you get scared," Alekos asked warmly.

"Not one bit, I'm just skimming through what to say," Elrin responded with his head high.

"Oh, contemplating are you?" Alekos played along.

"No," Elrin admitted, shamefully. Alekos chuckled and then rubbed Elrin's head, "Come on," he instructed.

Jada was in front of her home; her mother was visible inside, but her father must have been out working in the fields. As Alekos approached, Jada looked up, distracted from her play.

"Hello Jada, how are you today?" Alekos asked politely. She peered up at him, squinting slightly from the sun. "I'm good, did you want my mom?" she responded.

"I'm glad to hear you're doing good," Alekos continued, "I was just wondering if you would like to join me and Elrin on our way to Loin's." Suddenly, her face grew to that similar to the one Elrin expressed earlier. She, too, knew what he was offering.

"Sure!" she exclaimed, rushing into her house to tell her

mother, "I'll be back— going to Loin's!" Her voice shouted, half-hyperventilated, expressing her excitement as she broke back out of the house.

Both she and Elrin were masked in exhilaration as they waddled after Alekos like a mother hen and her chicks. Loin was the butcher. He roasted the most captivating, most delicious boar legs in all the land. They were simply to die for.

When they got there Loin was turning a pig over his fire. The rich, savory aroma of the pork sifting into the air made the atmosphere nearly edible. The kids ran to him making him turn, in surprise, from his work. He knew from their expression what they came for and smiled at Alekos when he saw him.

"How have you been holding up stranger? It's been a long while since you been in town," Loin asked as he unhooked two freshly roasted legs that hung loosely from the ceiling.

"Things have been going well for us, thanks for asking Loin," Alekos replied as he loosened the tie around the pigskin that jingled joyfully from his hip.

"No it's alright, this one's on me," Loin interrupted Alekos before turning to give the legs to the kids.

Alekos smiled and retired the sack but then suddenly something caught his eye. Something was moving in the bushes at the edge of the forest. He peered towards the brush, focusing attentively into the shadows, but saw nothing.

"Hey Loin," Alekos asked, before turning away from the forest. "Did you hear the howling last night," Alekos continued after he was sure the children's attention was stuck on the feast.

"There haven't been canines in these forests for years," Alekos stated in confusion, "Am I wrong?"

Loin turned once more from his pig and leaned slowly towards Alekos before speaking softly. "I heard the howl too, you weren't mistaken. Some of the king's hunters passed through the village already this morning."

He lowered his voice even more and took another step closer to Alekos. "It sounded like a lycanthrope from the mountains," Loin murmured as he leaned in.

"I thought the same myself, but what would make them flee the mountains and come into our forests?" Alekos questioned.

"You know, as I do, our ancestors came through those mountains to live here. Let's hope what caused that move isn't what's causing this," Loin finished as he turned back to his roast.

Alekos then turned to Elrin. "Elrin, don't be out late; go inside before the sun goes down. I mean it. I have to go," Alekos softly instructed when Elrin looked up. Elrin nodded obediently but returned his attention once again to the delicious meat. He was enjoying himself.

Chapter 2

It was getting near sundown before Alekos got back to his home; the sound of life seemed to be dwindling in the air as the transition to night approached. Caterina was outside hanging clothes from the line that tightly stretched between the house and the barn near Alekos' trail. He called her name as he arrived, and she turned and smiled before setting her work down to meet him.

"Oh my, you reek of Loin's extravagant meat. Did you bring some home?" she interrogated.

"Of course," Alekos smiled as he brought up his leather bag that emitted the aroma of the food.

"Fantastic," Caterina declared and reached forward to take the bag from him.

"The king's hunters passed through the town this morning," Alekos said, interrupting her conquest to make dinner. "I think they're hunting thropes," he continued.

Caterina's face twisted in confusion before she spoke, "Impossible, canines don't roam these forests."

Alekos released the bag for her, but continued, "I know, I was wondering the same, but even you heard the howl last night."

There was a brief pause before it was interrupted by a raindrop striking Alekos' cheek, and thunder roaring off into the distance. Caterina flinched slightly at the rumble before motioning for them to go inside.

"Do you really think there are thropes in the forests?" Caterina asked as she lit a candle near the doorway. Alekos sat down in a chair that waited patiently near the table.

"I don't know. It's bizarre that they would travel out of the mountains, even with the storm," Alekos murmured.

Caterina walked quietly over to the wall and peered out the window that was fixated towards the village. "There hasn't been any message of an attack, or a sighting either," Alekos continued. His gaze was set on Caterina, who glanced back at him.

"I'm sure everything will be fine," he reassured her when seeing the worry in her face.

"Yeah," she smiled, though her expression exposed her true feelings. She strode from the window into the chair that eagerly awaited her arrival next to Alekos.

Alekos studied her as she sat quietly, he knew she was worried. "Don't worry, the king's men will handle everything. They've all been through a lot tougher things, especially the king," he encouraged her, hoping to see her calm. Caterina looked up to Alekos and opened her mouth to speak, but then she stopped and held her gaze on him still worried.

"What's worrying you?" Alekos questioned her, "you're normally more confident than I am." She gazed at him before sighing, "Alekos… there's something I need to tell you," Caterina began, "when you were a—"

Suddenly a piercing scream screeched through the window, a woman was in trouble. Alekos sprung from his chair to the window to hear more shouts and cries coming from the village, and smoke, barely visible through the rain, emitting from town.

"Stay here," Alekos ordered as he rushed to the door. He swung the door open and took off in the direction of the village.

"Be careful," Caterina called after him as he vanished

through the threshold.

Relentlessly, he dashed forward as the rain pelted him on all sides, drenching him completely, but his mind was focused on the village. The closer he got, the quieter the village got. Immediately his mind went to Elrin. He needed to get there, and his determination drove him to run faster.

When he got to the village the sight crushed him. The village was desolate and tranquil, the rain already smothered the few huts that had been ablaze. One of the homes was Jada's. Dreadfully, he looked for signs of whom or what attacked. However the rain had embellished the ground with puddles and there was no luck or chance with finding tracks.

Alekos strode over to Jada's home, hoping for a sign, and the closer he got the more he noticed the destruction set upon it. The door was noticeably kicked in, and though severely seared the interior looked as though someone, or something, was searching for something.

Erratic, he rummaged for clues, but the fire's damage was done. It was hopeless. He stepped outside an animal could be seen among the rain on the far side of the village from him. Alekos looked keenly towards it, trying to make out what it was, but then it vanished into the woods behind it.

Without thinking, instinct drove him in the direction of the creature, however something caught his eye as he neared the woods. An arm appeared from the inside of Loin's shack. It was covered in blood. Alekos changed direction and ran towards the arm looking for its owner. As he neared, he could see that it was Loin himself. Alekos sped up and fell beside him as he arrived.

"What happened?" Alekos stammered looking for where the blood was coming from. Loin looked up towards Alekos, his face sketched with dread, and grabbed Alekos' arm. He tried to speak but he could only manage a gasp; his lung had been punctured.

"Loin, where is everybody?" Alekos knew he wasn't going to live much longer, but he needed to know if the villagers were still alive.

Loin pulled Alekos closer to him and opened his mouth, "Save… them," he gasped painfully, and, as the words escaped his lips, his arm dropped, his finger pointing towards the mountains.

Alekos held onto Loin's chest as his eyes slowly closed. His chest sunk in as his soul escaped in the last breath. Alekos' emotions shivered down his spine as anger and remorse strangled each other amid the rest. He gripped the fabric that soaked against Loin's lifeless body before standing and letting out a roar. He looked up, and with burning amber eyes he stared bitterly towards the mountains.

However, Alekos was clueless about what he was facing, so he knew he needed to be prepared. He headed to the blacksmith's shop, but as he expected it appeared to have been looted. He stepped into the threshold and looked down to see the door cleaved into two separate pieces. He was surprised that the door survived the fire earlier that day.

There was a table that the tongs and jigs laid, and tools were scattered across the floor. The forge burned a dead fire. It was completely solemn. A chest was torn open beside it, completely scavenged, and the hooks on the walls that previously hoisted bracers were unhinged and bare. Everything was barren and destroyed, even the shelves on the wall. Then just before he lost hope, Alekos noticed a hole in the ground just beneath a piece of the door; it was artificial, so he knew something was there.

Alekos bent down and pushed the door away and felt the ground, beneath the dirt it was hollow. With haste, he felt around looking for a handle he could use to lift what seemed to be a trap door.

Shortly afterward he was not left disappointed. What had appeared to be a root in the ground actually was the handle, and, as he lifted it open, the door expressed its years of neglect. The hinges creaked with old age, and dust filtered into the room nearly choking Alekos. He let out a cough and waved his hand through the air to make out what was stored inside.

As the dust cleared a box slowly appeared, and immediately Alekos withdrew it from its old home beneath the ground. The box, too, expressed its abandonment, as it groaned while Alekos pried the lid open. Much to his dismay, what laid inside slightly disappointed him; it was only a slingshot and a pouch.

Partially let down, he refocused himself on the villagers and took it. There was no room to be picky and he would be otherwise unarmed if he had not stumbled across it in the first place. He fastened the pouch to his waist and tucked the slingshot into his pants as he walked outside. He then turned once more to face the mountains.

Fear clumped deep down inside, but his courage weathered the storm and, with determination, he persevered. Without any other means of transportation, he dashed forward into the woods. By now the rain was dying and the view in front of him cleared mostly. The elements were on his side, but it would still take till nightfall before he got to the mountains. However, he planned to catch up to them before they got there.

The rain hushed, exposing the sun, and the orange rays of its setting glistened through the trees. It wasn't quite dark yet, but Alekos knew it was coming soon. He refused to stop and fight through the wet vegetation to make a torch, so he rushed on forward braving the inevitable darkness. Soon after he felt a sense of relief as the mountains could be seen nearing through the trees.

Then, as if by fate, the sun settled beyond the mountains, flooding the forest in shadows. He could hear commotions and see the flicker of fire in the distance beyond the trees. Abruptly, his paces halted to a silent lurk, and he spied quietly as he peered around the trees.

The light he saw came from a cave that broke into the mountain's edge. He studied carefully among the shadows and saw only one man. He definitely was not from around here. Then another appeared beside him. "*Who are they? What do they want?*" Alekos asked himself as he watched them murmur from one to the other. Their dark obsidian-colored plate armor reflected the dancing illumination from within the cave.

Suddenly, Alekos saw a shadow move across the cave entrance. "Maybe this is where everyone is being held captive," he thought. He scattered his thoughts for a plan, they were armed and he was outmatched and outmanned. There was no telling the experience they had, especially if they kidnapped the whole village. His heart's pace quickened, and he skimmed through the ideas that blurred through his mind. He went to steady his shaken hand on his waist, and it fell onto the pouch he found with the slingshot. He pulled the string that held it closed and pulled out what felt like a marble inside.

Alekos gazed at it, and the firelight exposed the mysteriously mystical object. It looked clear with a swirling purple fog suffocating the inside, and as the fire danced in the background, every so often red swirls danced back as if correlating a routine with the fire. Beyond his gaze, his peripherals caught the two men separating, ending their conversation.

Without thinking, he pulled the slingshot from behind him and, after placing the projectile inside the pocket, he drew it to a full length and aimed. If he had it just right he could knock him unconscious and not draw the attention of the other.

When he released it, the bullet raced across the distance bashing directly in the soldier's skull. Immediately, the ball exploded as it collided. A dark plum fog consumed his head, and the man dropped to the ground.

He was unconscious.

Instantaneously Alekos withdrew another one noticing that the other man's attention was caught. He quickly loaded it into the pocket, fumbling only slightly, as the man charged at him. Alekos knew if the man got near him it would be a fight between life and death.

Without hesitation, he promptly raised the slingshot. He aimed for a brief moment and released it. The piercing whistle of the marble cut through the air, and a split second later converged with the man's chest. Magically the man blasted back as the marble shattered on his chest. The purple haze that exploded dissipated with the blast of air that immediately retaliated.

Alekos stood half shaken and half bewildered as his heart pounded. His mind was racing, but moments later it was interrupted by a crushing sound, followed by movement, behind him. He turned just in time to see another man charging at him, sword drawn. It was too late for the slingshot. He dropped it quickly and dove beneath the vibrating echo the sword made as it was slung over his head.

Alekos turned to see his relentless opponent already coming back at him, this time swinging down at Alekos' recovering body. With no time to stand Alekos leaped weakly to the side, crashing on his back. Fear gripped his throat as the sword dug into the ground, inches from his feet, where he had just sat.

Without thinking he kicked the sword as the opponent withdrew it, nearly disarming the assailant, and jumped to his feet. As his rival regained control of the blade, he began to charge. Alekos mindset quickly switched from fear to a determination to live, while focusing back on the villagers.

Fury had built inside him now, and Alekos kicked forward. Colliding his foot with the rushing enemy's chest. To Alekos' luck, the man fell back dropping his sword.

Now the odds were even.

The assailant stumbled quickly back up, ignoring his sword, and his vision locked on Alekos. His eyes gleamed pure evil from the crevice in his helmet, and the fire in the background danced on his armor. Alekos quickly noticed that no metal was around his neck.

The soldier swung forward clenching his fists. His swing was fast, and Alekos barely had time to lean out of the way before another came at him. He put his arms up, but his successful block resulted in his forearms clashing with the enemy's metal bracers, and the speed and strength of the blow knocked him back.

Alekos stumbled until his back collided with a tree. Thinking quickly, Alekos ducked under the next swing and scooped the man onto his back and commenced with punching his rival's throat. After a few swings, Alekos knew to stop. The man was immobile. He sighed as he looked around with his heart pounding and arms throbbing.

He paid no attention to the bruises on his forearms as he got up and retrieved the unconscious man's sword and sheath. After, he then turned to pick up the slingshot he had tossed aside. As he picked it up, his thoughts momentarily went to the collateral damage they previously caused before refocusing on the cave.

Chapter 3

After ensuring there were no more men outside, Alekos passed the clearing between the trees and the cave before pausing again to listen for sounds of them inside. Confident there were no more, he peered around the corner into the cave. He was relieved when he saw that there were only three places set up around the fire where the men were to lie that night.

Alekos stepped inward and looked around. The ceiling was low and the room was scattered with stalagmites, though no signs of life. There appeared to be another passage in the back of the cavern, however, so he set forth in the direction. He was close; he knew it. As he edged his way towards the back he stepped softer, listening carefully for signs of movement. It was quiet, so he made his way vigilantly into the passage. Crevices were littering the ceiling and walls, embellishing the hall with a graceful moonlight, yet the air still slithered ominously down Alekos' back.

Slowly, the flicker of fire danced off the walls as he crept further in, and as it faded from view, suspense began to oscillate. His heart thudded loudly within his chest as he was showered momentarily in the moonlight, and when he was swallowed in darkness, his ears echoed from the blood that pulsated in his ears.

It was quiet, really quiet.

Something was not right.

Suddenly there was a sound of movement behind him, but, as he turned, only the shadows of the cavern peered back with malevolence. He peered into the darkness, carefully looking for something, anything, and yet nothing. He was becoming paranoid. Then he heard something else. Was it a muffled cry?

Alekos turned back in the direction he was first heading and hastily scurried in the direction the sound came from. As he edged closer, the sound grew louder. The desperation curdled in the cry, pleading through its muffle. Then, abruptly, it came to a halt; the cavern was lifeless. Alekos stopped short, and then fear strangled his gut; burning his mind with the images of what happened to the village.

"*Are they dead?*" He wondered.

His grip tightened around the sword as Alekos took off in a run, too fast to count the cascades of light that flashed past him or hear the scuttle of something tainted scampering away. Then rapidly, as he turned a corner, light flooded the cavern. The whole room was illuminated by a massive hole in the ceiling that towered high above him, exposing the moon amongst an eerie sky. The giant room Alekos stumbled across resembled that of a hive. The walls were bowled as they climbed high, smothered in enormous cavities and they glimmered almost magnificently in the moonlight.

Unaware of the changing texture of the cavern walls that suddenly became white, Alekos intruded inwards, desperately looking for the source of the agonizing cry that now laid in slumber. It was not long before the sound of trickling ricocheted in Alekos' ear. He turned to the sound, which came from an opening in the hive wall, and stared meticulously into the shadowed hole.

Then his eyes adjusted, but as the sight inside came to him, his stomach twisted immediately he felt sick. His gut churned and heated as the sight burned into his memory. It was a king's knight spun in a web, much like a spider does to his prey. His stomach had been gashed opened, and his insides were relinquished and missing. Blood relentlessly sifted from beneath his vacant ribcage, and more trickled down his pale white face. Alekos could see the man's desperation to live through his bloodshot, sunken eyes on his face.

Alekos turned away, nearly vomiting, as his stomach rose up repulsed, and his vision became fuzzy momentarily until he heard another sound. He was not alone.

His eyes scattered across the hive, but he could see nothing. Then as the suspense climbed his throat and the pounding of his heart echoed in his ear, he heard a cry. "Help meee..," the cry was bloodcurdling, but Alekos knew who it was.

It was Elrin.

Immediately losing focus on his surroundings, he broke off in the direction of the sound. "Elrin!" Alekos called out, his voice reverberating on the cavern walls. He entered the passage he heard Elrin come from and called out again. There was nothing, but he kept on forward. Then he heard Elrin exhaustively cry, "Alekos!!"

He turned the corner to see a fire flickering on the walls at the end of the cavern hall. His muscles burned as he stretched his stride, and as Alekos reached the turn his previous fear clumped in his chest again, suffocating him. It was just then he realized why the cavern seemed brighter. The walls were embroidered with webs, and, across from him, multiple bodies embroidered the walls. He saw Elrin, along with the other villagers, and a couple of knights, all fastened to the wall. Worst of all, they weren't alone.

Alekos stared in horror at the creature's massive body. It had a woman's bare torso and a massive spider body. Its feet clicked on the cavern floor as she swung her amethyst colored torso around to face him, whipping her long black hair as she snapped her head. The face was sketched with eight black eyes, which gleamed crimson in the fire, and as she opened her mouth to screech, her fangs elongated.

She rushed forward at him and unfastened her hands to reveal the tremendously sharp fingers it bore. Alekos raised his sword, but she moved quicker and immediately was there. It was too late to avoid her, or even attempt a swing because she collided into him. He ricocheted into the wall behind him but kept a firm grip on his sword. The force of the impact saved him from the adhesive wall and he hit the ground.

With little time to react to her approach, he pointed his

sword out, and a cry let out. The sword plunged her stomach and, in agony, her front two limbs collapsed to the floor. She swung once more, slightly slicing Alekos, but her efforts were futile as she laid there bleeding. She was dying.

Then suddenly her chest expanded, as air filled her lungs one last time, and she opened her mouth to let out a bloody shriek.

That was not good. Alekos knew he had to hurry. Ignoring the blood, now spilling from his arm, he ran over to the closest person to him, the town drunk. His drunken face was frozen in horror, but, as Alekos cut him free, his breath returned revitalizing him. Alekos paid no mind as he continued to cut everyone free, as quickly as he could.

Elrin was the first to leap at Alekos, wrapping his arms as tightly as he could to Alekos' neck. The boy was horrified. "We need to go," Alekos whispered as he placed him down, still focused on the level of danger that everyone was still in. Instinctively, one knight stepped forward pointing towards the passage opposite from which Alekos came, "The beast brought us in from that direction."

Alekos nodded and motioned for everyone to follow the knights. "You guard the front," he ordered the knights. "I'll cover the rear," Alekos continued, and immediately more shrieks, fiercer than the one he just heard, reverberated against their surroundings. "Run," he stammered.

The knights led the way through the passage with everyone quickly following from behind, and Alekos shuffled slowly backward, looking for the shadows of the monsters. The sounds of them flooding closer raised the horror that pounded in his chest, and sweat beaded off his forehead.

Then, suddenly something grabbed at his waist, he turned to see the blacksmith who had grabbed the slingshot and was loosening the sack from Alekos' waist. "Now is not the time for this," Alekos demanded, "Run!" The man continued, however, and looked Alekos in the eyes, "No you run, I will follow. Trust me," the man replied.

Alekos peered anxiously into the blacksmith's eyes, but then submitted. "Make it back alive," Alekos insisted worriedly. The man replied with only a slight nod, but then beckoned

Alekos to leave, "Hurry!"

Without objection, Alekos turned and chased after the group. As he reached a turn in the path, the tunnel opened wider, and he could see the group ahead through the flooding moonlight that scattered the hall. Moments later he heard the haunting screeches behind him followed by an incendiary roar. Firelight consumed the hall from whence they came and immediately Alekos halted in his path. He turned around to see the bend reflecting the raging ember, and then moments later a shadow flickered across it.

Alekos gripped his sword, preparing to fight, but then the blacksmith came running around the corner, his large body thundering with each step. "Go," he yelled forward.

Relieved, Alekos turned to race to the finish. Smoke funneled behind them, and the angry cries of the beasts slowly faded in the distance.

The group was huddled together behind the knights, who stood, sword drawn, towards the entrance as they reached the exit. They suddenly all relaxed, and a sense of relief filled the air. Alekos and the blacksmith were safe, and smoke was pummeling gracefully from the entrance behind them. It seemed that everything was over.

Alekos sheathed his sword, and Elrin once more ran at Alekos, gripping him tightly around the waist. Alekos went to smile, but a piercing pain shot up his left side. His arm was nearly numb from the excruciating gash in his arm. He brushed it off and rubbed Elrin's hair before turning to the knights.

"We need to get to the king," Alekos beckoned eagerly, "He needs to know what's going on."

The closest soldier looked to him before speaking, "There are three horses beyond the trees. One of us can ride ahead to warn the king." Alekos studied the words as they parted his lips, his head heavy, "Send for more soldiers and a carriage to transport everyone. I'm going to need a horse too, there is still someone in the village. I must go to her." His desperation shook in his voice, so the knight agreed.

"I'll have Sir Skoler stay with the group as we ride. I'm Garette by the way, thank you for saving our lives," the knight stated.

Alekos just nodded as Sir Garette directed everyone to the horses that were not far at all. Alekos immediately mounted one when they approached. Then he turned to face the crowd.

"I'll meet you all in the castle by morning; please be safe," he said wearily yet resolute.

Alekos looked up into the sky, and the moon shined down vibrantly towards him filling him with courage. He turned the reigns towards the village and kicked off.

The wind raced across his chest and brushed his hair back. The cooling touch of the icy air singed his wound as though the wind was purposely gripping it with its freezing touch. Slowly his head became heavy and his mind blurred as he rode. He constantly shook his head as he tried to stay awake, however, the pain in his arm slivered up his shoulder and whispered exhaustion into his ears as his eyes slowly closed.

Suddenly a man was standing over him with his sword drawn swinging down at him. Alekos reached out to stop him, pressing his hand against his chest, but it was too late. The sword plunged into his heart, and suddenly Alekos woke to realize he was in the village. He had fallen off the horse, who was now innocently chewing grass next to him.

Alekos grabbed the reins and exhaustively hoisted himself onto his feet; the pain of his gash now seared his whole body. He needed to get to Caterina before anything happened to either of them. He looked back to the sky to see the moon still accompanying his journey. After a relentless and agonizing effort, he pulled his way onto the horse and whipped the reigns, clicking his tongue. Obediently, the horse began to trot gently as if sympathizing with Alekos' pain.

They moved through the solemn village, and the lifeless body of Loin could be made out in the darkness of the twilight. Alekos turned his head, trying to keep the weight of the night off him. He tried to focus on the peace that still endured the tragedy. The night settled peacefully in respect to those lost, even the horses' trots seemed to be muted. Moments later Alekos was heading up the trail to his hermitage.

There was a lit candle inside, which came to a huge relief to Alekos. It wasn't until now that he fully appreciated the solemn solitude the house conducted as it settled humbly afar from the village. He tumbled off the horse and staggered towards the door as though drunk. He fumbled for the handle and pulled, but as he opened the threshold to his abode his heart shattered.

Everything was turned over as though someone had been searching for something, and Caterina was nowhere to be seen. His chest became heavy, and his heart climbed into his throat. He looked around eagerly hoping for a clue, averting his gaze hysterically about. He didn't want to believe it. Alekos stumbled inwards and hit the ground. "Caterina!"

The floor beneath him creaked, and a voice broke out, "Alekos?" Alekos cracked a smile of relief and shattered a tear happily. He knew it was Caterina. The floor beneath him opened up and Caterina rose from beneath, but her gaze quickly froze on his arm.

She jumped, from beneath, towards Alekos, and, as he raised his arms cheerfully to hug her, he collapsed. His feet crumbled from beneath him, and his vision quickly faded to black. The last thing he saw was Caterina rushing towards him, her face in horror, and his heart pounding too loudly to hear anything else.

"What do you mean he escaped? You told me this would work. You told me we'd get him," the poisonous voice of the shaded man hissed violently towards the oracle.

"There are other ways, we can still get him before he gets to you," the man trembled in reply, his voice cracking as it shook.

"You've shown me how to make my army," the harsh voice of Kojax scolded, "You have one more chance! One more! Get them through the hole, or you'll be no longer needed." The bloody face of the oracle vividly expressed his fear.

Chapter 4

Voices and movement clamored into Alekos' ear and abruptly he woke. He sat up quickly and a small, soft hand met his chest. “Rest,” said the voice gently. Alekos gazed with blurred vision at the woman, who appeared to be young. He blinked trying to focus his vision on her, but his head once more became heavy and he slowly fell back to his pillow.

Alekos looked in the direction of the ruckus that stirred him. He could see the long room he was in. Multiple beds were lining the walls on both sides, and small tables sat between each of the cots. Then suddenly his memories rushed back to him. “Where am I?” He sat up once more revitalized. However, when he looked around the young woman was gone.

Alekos shook his head from its daze and twisted his legs off the bed. As his feet positioned themselves on the ground, the door opened. It was Caterina. She turned her head and nodded to someone, and then feet could be heard pattering. Momentarily, the beast he had slain flashed into his head, but as the face of Elrin thrillingly revealed itself from beside Caterina the memory dissipated from his thoughts.

Elrin's face lit up in glee, and he raced towards Alekos as Caterina slowly followed along with a few others. Alekos' stomach twisted as he prepared for socialization, but he opened his arms in time to catch Elrin jumping into them. "We were so worried! You had been poisoned when the monster attacked you, and when you were brought in, your skin was changing colors! I was so worried. Are you ok?" Elrin stammered as his words clumsily stuck together.

"Slow down," Alekos chuckled as he looked at his now bandaged arm. Alekos felt a cool droplet hit his arm as a tear broke free from Elrin's face. Alekos held him close as the others gathered. Jada and her mother stood and bowed their heads in gratitude, but Caterina spoke first.

"I saw the king's horse and knew to take you here. You had me worried sick, I didn't even take the time to shut the door," her voice uttered the sorrow she felt, but her face illuminated her relief. "Thank you," Alekos replied, "I'm glad everyone is safe."

"I wanted to be by your side all night, but they wouldn't let me," Elrin sniffled as he wiped his nose. Alekos nudged Elrin's chin with his curled index finger and smiled. "It's fine. I'm fine," Alekos reassured him before looking up and changing the subject.

"What about the creatures in the mountains?" Alekos inquired.

The blacksmith spoke next, "Sir Skoler and Garette took a squad of soldiers to investigate and kill any that survived the fire. They should be returning by morning, if not by this night's end."

"How long have I been sleeping?" Alekos murmured to Caterina.

"Almost a whole day," she replied softly. "They're preparing a feast now in the hall."

Alekos pondered momentarily before attempting to stand. "Can everyone wait for me outside?" he asked, opening his arms to exemplify that his torso was bare of clothing. Caterina nodded and took Elrin by the hand to lead him out. Jada's mother stepped forward and hugged Alekos quickly, "Thank you," she whispered before turning to guide Jada out, who bowed her head shyly.

"Wait for just a second Marcus," Alekos spoke as the blacksmith started to turn.

"Yes?" he responded.

"How did the fire start," Alekos asked after he picked up his leather tunic from the table beside his bed. He swung his arms through the holes to slide it on, and he turned to reach for the sheathed sword he had looted.

Marcus looked momentarily at Alekos before reaching into his pocket. He pulled out the bag that held the slingshot marbles before speaking. "These are not just normal bullets," he started, "The magic within them is phenomenal. This bag never runs out of ammo, for every time the orb shatters it renews itself within the pouch. However, the most mysterious thing about them is they stimulate your thoughts. In this case I wanted the webs and spiders to burn so when it shattered it consumed its surroundings in a fiery ember. I've had this locked away because it is a very powerful weapon and dangerous if in the wrong hands. I'm just a blacksmith what do I know about magic."

Alekos gazed in awe at the pouch and thought back to the encounter with the soldiers. It made sense now. "That's spectacular," Alekos exclaimed, "I didn't know how it worked, but, without it, I wouldn't have been able to save anyone."

Marcus smiled and looked down at the pouch in his smoke-stained hands. "That is why I want you to have it," he replied, pulling out the slingshot from his back pocket. "Thank you for saving my life," he smiled as he handed it to Alekos and nodded his gratitude.

"What-- really?" Alekos stuttered astoundingly; he couldn't believe it.

"Of course," Marcus smiled, "Just be careful; don't knock yourself out." He chuckled as he turned to exit the room.

"Thank you," Alekos murmured as he gazed down at the new gift. He couldn't believe how disappointed he was when he first looked at it. Now, it shined brighter than everything he'd ever seen in his mundane life. Alekos placed it on the bed beside him to slide on his boots and then mounted the pouch to his waist along with his sheath. After tucking his trousers into his boot, he stood up, armed his hips, and started to walk towards the hall.

As soon as he stepped out into the hall, the ruckus hushed. Then a crescendo of whispers began to grow, each one crawling and scratching desperately for Alekos. However, just before his head overflowed from the words, the king interrupted by calling Alekos to his presence.

Alekos turned from the crowd and headed towards the direction of the king. A large and long table extended the length of the hall, and the aroma of freshly prepared food lavishly drifted off from them. Eyes locked on Alekos as he brushed past them, their hard gaze lashed their many unasked questions. As he got to the king he knelt before the steps up to the throne, and the king beckoned for him to rise and sit beside him. Alekos looked up to him in surprise and stood to ascend the three steps that separated them.

As Alekos took the first step the king stood and met him hand outstretched. Alekos took his hand and was pulled in for an embrace. "You did a fine job," the king stated, fully expressing his gratitude as he separated from Alekos still holding his hand, "You saved my men, and showed your allegiance and passionate devotion to your fellow townsmen and the kingdom. For this, I am truly grateful to be in your presence." He let go of Alekos' hand and brushed his hand through the air to motion Alekos to an open seat at his table.

"Thank you very much, I appreciate that," Alekos replied reservedly, as he sat beside the king. The recognition, he felt, was undeserving.

The king motioned for the maidens to bring them food and wine and then turned to Alekos to continue. "You were lucky to live, you know that. Those beasts are unlike anything my men have ever encountered. My best doctors had no experience with the poison your body ingested. They say you would have been dead if your spirit wasn't so strong," the king explained as the food was brought to the table.

The smell was extravagant, and Alekos' stomach immediately reciprocated with a loud growl as the large roasted chicken, sweet buttery corn cobs, and a large bowl of peas was placed in front of him. "By all means," the king chuckled, hearing Alekos' stomach, "Feast!"

Obediently, Alekos respectfully and neatly gathered food on his plate, having been raised properly by a woman. Once he was finished, the king dove into the buffet, grabbing the corn and peas with his large round hands and ripping off the part of the chicken he wanted. His manners were grotesque, but he was king. It was still a relief and a distraction, as it was as humorous as it was enjoyable to watch.

"If I was mistaken, I'd say you were hungrier than me, my lord," Alekos joked as he took his first bite. The flavor was exquisite, and his taste buds melted in their satisfaction.

The king let out a hard laugh, "Please call me Crewel," he stated as he smiled. "And as slim as I am, I enjoy my food," Crewel teased. He wasn't all that slim, but he was not large either. He had somewhat the body that a stereotypical king ought to have.

"I see that, and Crewel?" Alekos questioned, "I've always wondered about that."

"Well you know what happened," he paused, "my brother liked to call me that."

Alekos continued to eat but noticeably slowed down his chewing. After a moment he spoke. "Forgive me for asking, if this may offend, but how is your father?"

Crewel put his food down and finished his mouthful, but his face was etched sternly. "I know. It looks bad. Hundreds of years go by, and our line has always reigned without problems since the Battle through Dead Man's Gorge. We fought for our peace and serenity, as the story goes, blah blah blah," he started. Alekos could not tell if it was the emotions or the wine, but they did not mix with this topic. "I could tell you how unfair it is, but, truth be told, what happened took a huge toll on him. The first king to be a widower, and now I'm afraid if he didn't have me then he wouldn't make the effort to live," Crewel retorted.

"He was a good king, but luckily we have another one to take his place," Alekos spoke and raised his chalice to lift the mood, "I'm sorry about your losses, I lost my parents as well. Life has its cruel ways of making us stronger."

"Aye."

The king raised his goblet to meet Alekos' but did not return to eating. Alekos did not notice though, he was too busy ingesting his meal. The king, instead, was keenly studying Alekos. "So tell me," he spoke after a while, "What happened? I've heard what others had to say, but what did you see?" he questioned.

Alekos paused from eating, and wiped his face before turning to the king. "Wait, say what?"

"Last night," Crewel chuckled.

Immediately Alekos' mind revisited the night before, the images still vivid. He paused slightly, let out a breath, and cleaned his fingers on his trousers before setting his gaze on Crewel.

Alekos began telling him about the events of the night before. He embellished the recollection of his previous night with every emotion he felt and every vibrant detail of the images burned into his memory. He had not noticed, as he neared his finish, that he had caught the attention of most of the hall. Even the maidens slowed from their work to eavesdrop. By the time he finished, his heart was pounding louder than the previously raucous hall.

The last light of the evening sun bathed the silence for a few moments before life was restored when Crewel spoke. "Though the souls of one of my dearest knights and your village butcher have been torn from their bodies, you honor this kingdom and me with your bravery and courage. More lives would have been lost if it wasn't for you, and for this I thank you," he stated.

He spoke words of comfort, but even then Alekos could tell the king was at a loss for words. No one knew what was going on, not even the king. Alekos knew the beast he slew was not one anyone has ever seen before, and fear gripped everyone's hearts.

The king turned away from Alekos' lack of a verbal response, and turned to the crowd. "These forests have been our home for centuries, and now the spawn of evil is trying to enlighten the fear in our hearts and drive us from it. I will give every drop of my soul to preserve this kingdom, protect my people, and extinguish this filthy plague from within our boundaries!"

His words vibrated amongst the walls and regenerated the solemn atmosphere created by the silence. Everyone, including Alekos, seemed to take a satisfying breath that engulfed their innards with relief and comfort.

Finally, night fell into the hall and the flames of the

corridor blazed enviously against it. The king motioned for two of the knights to adjourn to the room behind his throne when the livelihood and chatter of the hall rejuvenated. Alone now, Alekos scanned the hall. To his relief, no one realized he was there anymore. He stood to head outside, but then he noticed someone.

It was the old man he rescued last night. Not once has this man spoken or acknowledge Alekos. Even now, and throughout Alekos' whole story, he gazed only momentarily, yet continuously at Alekos apathetically. His behavior was suspicious, to say the least.

In his bewilderment, Alekos strode over to the man, who sat in a booth in the far corner of the mess hall. When he arrived, the man stood from the booth. From beneath the hood of his robe his eyes stared coldly.

"There are things even you are blind of Alekos." He turned and strayed towards the door, the fabric of his robe trailing swiftly behind him.

As if an obedient dog to his master, Alekos followed the man, who drifted outside. He followed him through the massive threshold of the king's stronghold, across the courtyard, whose old fine grass has been trampled and ruined due to the many horseshoes that pounded heavily among it, and over to the stables before the man finally stopped.

"You can't stay here long," he warned ominously, finally breaking the silence, "It is not safe for you here."

Alekos shook from his trance, determined to figure out what was going on. "Why should I listen to you? You stay in your home every day. The village hardly knows you. What do you know about what is going on?" Alekos demanded while peering hard at the man.

"Far more than you could ever imagine, however, this is not the time to talk about this. Your life is far grander than you know and its sole survival determines everyone else's," the man continued, "Return home. Find your way to the Covenant."

"You make no sense; I will not run home like a child. If my life is so gravely important, why must I run and coward in my hermitage? I'm not you," Alekos retaliated, confused by the sudden approach. The man stepped forward while removing his hood, his face growing stern. "Your mother lost her life to protect you, and pity has it for you to carry this burden despite how naive you are to see the point. I will not waste my time explaining all this to you, like you shalt not do in your destiny. Go there now and let not her death be for nothing," he replied.

Offended, Alekos stepped forward and grabbed the man's robe, "My mother was killed by bandits," he scolded. Wearily the old man's eyes crinkled, studying Alekos, "I have spoken my words and that is all I will speak. If it is the truth you seek, you'll discover it upon doing what I say."

Alekos stood still unsure of the decision to make, however, after calming and acknowledging how old the man was, he let go of the man's robe. He opened his mouth to retaliate a response but was broken off by the shrill of a horse's neigh and the arrival of the king's men.

Their urgency was obvious in the midst of their commotion, and then Alekos saw what it was about. In a cage, crudely put together, they had a captive. Alekos could not make it out, but it shrilled inside and shook the walls of its tiny entrapment. A soldier met the head of the platoon, only murmurs could be heard. After taking a half step Alekos turned to look back, but the old man had vanished. After turning his gaze about, looking to see if he could find the man, he gave up and quickly paced over to the commotion, arriving just as the king stepped outside.

People could be seen gathering at the door. As their murmur grew louder, their curiosity could be heard drenching their voices. However, a soldier manned the door ensuring the privacy of the prisoner.

Chapter 5

"What is it," Crewel demanded eagerly, turning to glance at Alekos before looking back at the caravan.

"We went there and the caverns were clean. The fire left nothing but chars on the surface of the walls," the platoon leader responded.

The king's relief was expressed clearly with his sigh, but swiftly his attention tuned into the racket in the back of the assembly. "What is that noise?" he questioned uncomfortably, pacing towards the rattling cage.

"A survivor," the soldier responded as he hopped off his horse to follow Crewel. "It's an offspring of one of the creatures, but we have reason to believe it was abandoned due to its--"

"A survivor?! You left it alive?" the king broke off angrily.

"Sir it's lame; it's nearly defenseless. Doesn't seem to have a hint of wickedness to it," the man defended himself.

"They weren't defenseless when they defiled your brother, and scavenged him alive of his insides," Crewel's fury rose as he stepped nearer to the cage. Alekos quickly stepped over to the group.

"Sir, it was starved, dismembered and abused before we ever got to it. I thought maybe we could learn from--" the knight retaliated stuttering.

"We can learn from its dead corpse," the king broke off, unsheathing his sword and raising it towards the box.

"Wait!" His heart pounded heavily as Alekos exclaimed aloud. He was raised honorably and knew this was not right.

Crewel quickly turned in fury towards Alekos, "How do you hold pity for the beasts that tried to kill you too?" He fulminated.

"I hold no pity, nor do I support its welfare, but this creature is not what tried to slaughter me. Don't be rash, you know you can't punish one for the crime of another," Alekos burst out, defending the creature that now whimpered, "Open the crate. If it's as savage as you put it out to be, then I'll slay it myself."

Crewel stared firmly at Alekos, his sharp gaze chiseling the air, but Alekos did not cower. "You are truly remarkable to be able to forgive wickedness so easily, but this is on you," the king retorted apathetically.

"You cannot forgive nor condemn one whose actions and crimes are unknown," Alekos replied before turning to the soldier who curiously stood relieved. Alekos loaded his slingshot and drew back to aim at the crate, "You can open it."

Obediently, the knight climbed the wagon and went to fiddle with the chains of the cage, which stood up to his chest. After a clink, the chains rattled to the floor, and the crate door began to fall. As the crate door hit the floor, the man jumped off the wagon, and Alekos pulled his grip closer to his sight.

Caution was the last thing on his mind the instant the sight of the creature appeared before him. At first, its back was facing him. The creature's back was adorned with gashes similar to the ones on Alekos' arm, and it was shuddering as if stricken and frozen by fear. It slowly began to turn, as its feet clicked against the wagon floor, and revealed a gruesome sight.

When it fully turned Alekos noticed that it gripped tightly onto the remnants of its right arm, which had been noticeably ripped loose from his body. Once turned, the face exposed that it was a young male, but the details couldn't be made out. His arm dripped feverishly with blood, and he hunched over from the noticeable pain that lingered in his back. No wonder he was going crazy in the cage.

This one was not like the rest, but why not? Alekos lowered his slingshot and spoke softly, "Come into the light. I won't hurt you as long as you have no intention of hurting me."

Crewel scoffed. He had no intention of believing its innocence, however, Alekos put no mind towards the king and stepped closer towards the crate. The young spider-like creature painfully crept tamely forward as well, obeying Alekos' whim. As its face became visible beneath the moonlight, Alekos' heart sank.

Beneath the wounds of his face over his right eyes there was a mark. Alekos stepped back alarmed, and shook his head. As the creature crept closer Alekos could see it clearly, he wasn't mistaken. That was Elrin's birthmark!

"What is it?" The king intercepted when Alekos expressed his alarm. Not wanting to tell the king of the coincidence he replied, "Nothing. I'm just disgusted by his state of being. He's in no shape to be sentenced now."

"I'll be the judge of that," the king retorted stepping forward towards the creature. Immediately the beast turned to him and, upon noticing the sword and anger the king bore, and let out a curdling screech defensively.

"Why you little," Crewel took a step back and raised his sword to slay the creature, which was unable to move away. A ball of distress regurgitated in Alekos' throat as he thought on his feet.

"No!" He cried aloud.

Alekos raised his slingshot swiftly and turned it to the creature as Crewel swung his sword down. He released it praying for his idea to work, and as the purple smoke consumed the young male's body the king's sword slung down through it. A painful shriek let out and a thud was heard as Crewel's sword became stuck with its rival.

Slowly the smoke dissipated, but the beast was gone. The king's sword had become stuck in the wagon. Crewel turned to Alekos and released his grip on his sword.

"What did you do?" He interrogated as he approached Alekos fiercely.

"I rid you of the burden Crewel, you had no right determining it fate," Alekos retaliated, his voice firm.

"Is it dead?"

"Hardly," Alekos replied. His face was stern yet vacant. He could not lie, and he knew that consequences would be dealt unto him.

The king turned in anger and swung back hitting Alekos in the face. As Alekos stumbled back, he was caught by two knights who held him. "You would spare the life of a beast that dares threaten your king! You disgrace my home with your dishonor," Crewel exclaimed furiously.

"He was scared and defenseless. I only spared him of a death by a coward," Alekos spat back.

Crewel opened his mouth but then tightened his face, pivoting in his place. "Arrest him," he snapped aloud as he quickly paced back to the hall. Alekos shook in anger but then something collided with the back of his head and conscious slipped away.

"How long till I can send them through?" Kojax hissed, approaching the weak and timid old man.

"Do you see where the hole is? Your family experiment with Arachne's barely made it. He's just been imprisoned, and the hole will descend in five days' time."

"You don't have five days!"

"If he doesn't find Megahte, he'll never stop you anyway. Just repeat your same experiment with some troops and send the beast with them," the oracle argued.

Kojax smirked and turned to leave. As he disappeared from view, a heavy metal door could be heard slamming shut.

The smell of feces woke Alekos up, and, when he opened his eyes, he immediately knew where he was. Everything about the jail was unwelcoming. The air was piercing. The floors and walls were forged of rough stone. The ground was covered in dry, painful prickly hay, and the reluctant bars stood lifeless between Alekos and his freedom.

He had been propped against the back wall, and he could tell he was dragged by the trails in the hay that branched from his feet. He pulled his feet towards him and rested his head against the wall.

He closed his eyes and tried to remember the strange dream he had, but it was a blur. Arachne, how could he dream a word he didn't know? He shook his head. It was just a dream and he needed to focus on getting out. His slingshot could work! Alekos reached to his back pocket, but he had seen it coming. They had stripped him of his weapons.

Just then, he heard galloping. Alekos hopped up and gazed out the jail window and a cold breeze met him as he peered. He noticed that he was right next to the stables. The noise was a scout on horseback. Alekos carefully eavesdropped and heard that the search for the beast was unsuccessful, and no villagers had reported disturbance either. Comforted, Alekos let out a sigh.

He turned quickly to investigate the jail; he had to get out and to the creature before it was found. He crossed the cell and began shaking the individual bars, but they were all fastened securely in their posts. Then suddenly a door down the hall could be heard opening, causing Alekos to step back innocently.

It was Crewel and a couple of guards.

"Where did you send it?"

Alekos smirked as though victorious, "Somewhere death awaits him by his choices. His fate is determined by his decisions."

"Don't you riddle me, either you tell me where it is or rot in this cell until we find it," Crewel snarled back.

"A wise king once said that life is a privilege, and we should fight those who deprive anyone else of their right to have it unless they solely deserve it. Crewel, you've staggered far off the path your father set for you," Alekos replied pitifully.

"It is in the king's power to enforce the peace and prosperity of the people. Anyone who tries to stop me is committing treason. You'll learn that soon enough," he snapped as he turned to leave.

"Only a cruel king could mock words, and use them to defend his actions!" Alekos hollered, mocking Crewel, before hearing the door slam shut.

Alekos backed up and chuckled to himself, and paced to the window where he saw the king striding. Disregarding that he was digging a hole he shouted, "All hail Crewel, deliverer of the horror and destruction of a cripple." Despite the insult, Crewel continued forward.

Alekos pivoted and kicked the hay frustratingly, but quickly looked up as he saw something glide past the jail towards the exit in the corner of his eye. He strode over to the gate to see a shadow vacating the doorway. Who was that? Alekos pondered.

He leaned closer and the door cracked open, and his weapons were guiltlessly rested on the floor. A guardian angel, Alekos praised. Not wanting to abuse his liberation, he swiftly equipped his weapons and strode out of the cell.

Alekos crept towards the exit as quietly as he could, but his boots quacked as they broke free from the sticky floor with each step. The closer he got to the doorway, the quieter he tried to be so he could keenly listen to the sounds outside, ensuring there were no guards.

After he was confident that his ears had not decided to betray him he sneaked around the doorway outside, leisurely poking his head around the corner. It now seemed to be a major design flaw that the jail was right next to the stable, but he still had to be careful. He looked around both for guards and for the person who had rescued him, but there was no one.

After making sure the area was clear, he made his way hastily into the stables and towards a horse. Again he looked around as he prepared the horse, saddling it properly while calming it. Just as he finished, a voice appeared behind him that made his heart skip a beat. He winced and turned, but was relieved to see Elrin.

"Where are you going?" He asked worriedly, "Are you going after the beast?"

Alekos scanned his words before kneeling to speak, "I must do this. I cannot explain it now, but I have to figure something out. I will return for you, but stay safe till then and tell no one you were here." He parted the hair from Elrin's face as he spoke, and then pulled him in to hug him.

Elrin gripped Alekos tightly and whispered, "You're not wrong." Alekos separated and looked at him puzzled. "No matter what anyone says, you're my hero, and no decision you can ever make can be wrong." Elrin finished and hugged Alekos again.

"Thank you," Alekos sighed as he closed his eyes, "But I have to go now."

Elrin obediently let go of Alekos and backed up. "I'll be waiting," he smiled before running back towards the hall.

Alekos turned back to the horse, and latched his arms to the saddle, but paused slightly thinking of what the old man had said and of the dreams he's been having. Can they be real? He thought. Realizing that just standing and pondering wouldn't get him anywhere, he shook his head and mounted the horse.

Suddenly a bellowing clash of lightning thundered in the distance as he climbed onto the horse. It came from the direction of the mountains, which, luckily, Alekos was heading opposite of.

Alekos clasped the reigns and struck them, cueing the horse to gallop. The horse obediently gave sovereign to Alekos and began to carry him towards the gate. This was to be the fun part.

Immediately guards retaliated by jumping from their posts; a few were in the gate tower and already unsheathing bows, and the rest raced towards their horses. There was no turning back now, so Alekos kicked the horse and beckoned for it to pick up speed.

The horse darted towards the gate that was now signaled to be closed, but it was too late. Alekos would make it in time, he knew it. Just then an arrow skimmed past his face, they'd gone lethal force. Hastily without thinking, Alekos withdrew his slingshot and a bullet before sending it spiraling towards the hunter. A cloud of purple followed by an unconscious bowmen appeared as Alekos raced out the gate.

However, he wasn't safe from harm. There was still another archer and two pursuers. He ducked as another arrow pierced the air, whizzing past him, and he directed the horse towards the woods. Another arrow struck his saddle, and he turned to see his pursuers tailing and catching up to him.

Then abruptly, the unthinkable happened, an arrow surged through his mount, crippling its front leg, and sending Alekos airborne forward off. He struck the ground but did not stop. His heart pounded, but it was his survival he cherished.

Alekos rolled to his feet and moved as fast as he could, each stride yearning to be longer than the next. He looked for a possible escape; there was no way he'd outrun two horses. The galloping behind him echoed in his ears, and the sound started to vibrate inside him. Then unexpectedly his body took over his actions, he moved quicker than he could think.

Immediately he withdrew two more marbles, his hand was still clasped tightly on the slingshot. He turned only momentarily to release one, only listening for a direct hit. It was successful, the man could be heard propelling off his horse. He then halted and swiftly turned, while raising his arms and squinting his eyes. Just as his aim aligned with his vision he released, and the second pursuer was detached from his mount as, he too, flew backward.

Alekos reached his arm out, as the horse continued to race towards him, and gripped the reigns swinging back onto the horse in one quick swoop. His heart still pounded, swelling his lungs and head with pulsating blood. His adrenaline was peaked, but he was safe and on his way towards his journey.

Chapter 6

By the time Alekos' heart slowed to a steady beat, and his horse trotted peacefully, it was high noon. The sun shafts cascaded beautifully in the trees and life swirled around him lively. It seemed as though things were back to normal, though he knew they weren't.

However, it didn't stop him from enjoying his surroundings. The past couple of days had been hectic, and the songs sung by the hymn birds resonated beautifully in his ears. He couldn't believe how pestering they use to be to him.

Alekos shifted side to side with each trot, and the rocking motion alleviated him of his thoughts, acquitting his ruminating. He bowed his head relaxed and set his gaze on the magical life of the forest floor.

It was the dirt devil he saw first, a bug that catches his prey by turning into dirt, and when something walks over him he consumes them. It had spiraled up his dirt like a twister, consuming a scarab that innocently trailed in the wrong direction. The devil condensed his body and scurried into the brush to hide. Ironically, the blades of grass it fled into came to life and wrapped around the creature, until it resembled a cocoon.

Alekos chuckled and scanned around more finding a fairy nymph snoozing peacefully beneath its mushroom shade. A clear curtain glittered along the edge of the mushroom cascading to the forest floor. If that curtain was to be disturbed the nymph would wake up immediately and vanish, a stunning defense mechanism.

The more he looked around the more lively the forest became. It was wondrous how mundane and magical animals alike could live in harmony. It would be preposterous, to most people, to live alongside a faun or a centaur, or any other humanoid creature. Even then Alekos wished for it, he couldn't imagine what was greater than magic. Even the trees seemed to be livelier in the forest than when surrounding mundane encampments.

He made it to a stream he had recognized, it led directly towards the village, so he knew he was getting close. He turned in the direction of the village, deciding to cross the bridge instead of treading the water when the time came.

Gold glimmers in the water caught his eye as the horse still carried him forward. He looked closer to see gold coins scattered across the stream bed, but he knew better than to dive in for it. The gold coins were actually gleets, round leeches that live in schools. They appear gold during the day so that if one unlucky person, or curious fish, decides to grab it, they can all latch onto their prey and kill it. The water was full of carnivorous monsters.

He whipped the reigns and motioned for the horse to pick up speed. He realized this wasn't a luxury trip; in fact, he needed to get there as soon as possible. The king's men would be looking for him, and possibly others as well.

Ahead he saw the bridge, lifelessly perched over the stream. However, he paused before he crossed it, his attention had converted to Loin. He never received a proper burial, so Alekos couldn't just leave his body there. He turned and trotted towards the village, slowing down the pace as he got closer.

As he neared, he heard a noise coming from the village. It was unfamiliar. Alekos hopped off his horse and calmed it into staying put, before ducking to draw nearer. He gazed out from behind a bush towards the village and saw that he was too late, the king's men were there searching.

In the middle of the village was a carriage, a blanket rested over a lump in the back. It was Loin, Alekos could recognize his bulging stomach anywhere. He turned to leave then suddenly his stomach growled. Luckily he wasn't within range to be heard but he was unmistakably still in a predicament.

There wasn't time to go hunting, build a fire, and then roast the meat. He knew Loin had some meat stored in his shack, but he was also unsure whether or not the soldiers emptied it. He pondered for a moment, but then realized his hermitage. He had just brought food there two days prior, which shouldn't have gone bad yet considering Loin's expertise.

So Alekos quickly diverted back to his horse, easing the horse's enthusiasm when he returned. It snorted at him when he hushed it from neighing, but then obediently calmed as Alekos hoisted upwards and directed the reigns in the direction of the bridge.

He was alleviated knowing Loin was going to get a burial, but his mind seemed more focused on quieting his stomach as he ventured for food. As he crossed the bridge, it croaked greeting him and groaned a farewell as the horse stepped off on the other side.

Immediately Alekos beckoned the horse to gallop down the trail towards his home. Moments later he could see it, and, luckily, no guards as well. He parted the horse at the entrance of the trail, where the empty hive of bees settled in tranquility. They had found a new home somewhere else.

Alekos jogged up the hill towards his hermitage and directly towards the door. It had been left open as Caterina mentioned, but it didn't seem like anyone had been there so he let himself in. As he expected the smell of the meat still radiated, he could track it as easily as a canine.

He chuckled when it led toward the cubby beneath the floor, Caterina had been eating it in his absence. When he withdrew the bag there was still enough inside to last him a few meals, so he was relieved. He took out a small strip of jerky that was inside and stood to go back out the door.

However, when he stepped near the threshold he could hear hooves thudding as they neared him. He peered out carefully to see two horsed soldiers coming up the trail towards his home. Alekos wanted to avoid a fight so he quickly turned and dashed into Caterina's room, sheathing the jerky back into the bag.

He shut the door behind him and quickly turned towards the window, but then he paused. The table in her room had a parchment lying on it with Caterina's handwriting inscribed onto it. Alekos edged closer to read it:

Go home.

His face curled in confusion, does she know something too? He didn't have long to think before he could hear the men entering the house, so he abruptly turned and exited the window.

As he hit the ground outside, he peeked around the house to see if both men had entered. They had, but he still didn't want to risk anything. Alekos turned towards the barn that was between the house and the direction he needed to head and quickly dashed towards it. He looked back as he made it just to make sure the men hadn't noticed, and then followed the walls around to the other side.

He could see the horse patiently waiting, so he took one more glance around the edge of the barn and then darted towards the horse. He gripped the reigns as he arrived and pulled the horse away from notice.

"Whew that was close," he chuckled to the horse, but only his stomach replied. After submitting to its demands he withdrew the jerky, mounted the horse and turned the reigns towards the direction he needed to go.

It was nearing dusk by the time Alekos approached his old home, his mind rushed back to the last time he was there. The only memory he had was the last time he saw his mother, which he found odd because he was eleven when it happened. He gazed at the ruined home, overgrown and part of nature now. It blended naturally with the surrounding woods that seemed just as hollow as it.

He dismounted and walked uneasily towards the decayed memories, the front door was still broken from its hinges. Alekos brushed aside the vines that hung loosely in the doorway and stepped inside onto the dust tarnished earthen floor. The crimson shafts of light cleansed the inside of its darkness, bathing the furniture that waited patiently in their graves until they too decayed with the home.

Alekos knelt beside the chair that his mother's blood had stained. He clenched his eyes to force back a tear as his throat strangled his breath, but then he heard a noise that awakened him back to reality. It came from the cubby that his mother had hidden him on the night of her death.

Alekos, though not alarmed, withdrew his sword ready to face what he had come for. He eased closely towards the compartment; with each step, the floorboards beneath him personified his approach. As he neared enough that the latch was within reach he leaned forward to unlatch it.

It unfastened with ease and the hidden door retaliated by stretching open, overjoyed with its newfound freedom. The burning crimson light of the dusked sun, eager to spread light beyond bounds hidden for years, flooded in and revealed the creature. It shivered in fear, now much more vulnerable, as it slunk backward from Alekos.

"It's okay, it's me. I won't hurt you," Alekos reassured the quivering ball that huddled in fear. The creature's shaking quickly decelerated, and his head tilted in interest. As his face leaned forward, and the light further bathed his face, his eyes glimmered like shiny obsidian. Innocence was seen in the eyes that once seemed wicked in another.

"Elrin?" Alekos asked as his face curled in curiosity.

The beast's lips quivered as he parted his lavender lips, "Kc-y-yes," he choked. It was noticeable that he hadn't spoken in a long while. "Who a-are you," he whimpered, his voice trembling.

Alekos' expression took back puzzled, "It's me Alekos. You know me. I've spent my life looking after you. Who did this, how did this happen?" Alekos' mind whirled as he tried to fathom what was going on. The real Elrin is still alive, but he is Elrin too?

"I don't know y-you," the Elrin responded.

Alekos opened his lips to persist but then halted. He knew it was not a pressing matter at the moment to stress the creature out further. "Are you hungry," Alekos smiled, "I have food."

The boy did not speak. Instead, he stepped closer, looking attentively at Alekos. "I'll be right back," Alekos reassured him, "Don't go anywhere." Alekos pivoted where he stood and paced towards the door. As he made it to the threshold the Elrin spoke once more, "Meat?"

Alekos stopped but only turned his head, "Yes," he smiled back though inside his mind battled furiously over the riddle of mystery. He turned back forward and stepped outside towards the horse, who patiently chewed stalks of overgrown grass. As he approached the horse it lifted its head to recognize him, but then returned to its dinner.

Alekos patted its neck and then opened the saddlebag on the horse. He had placed the food inside to keep himself from eating more than he needed. After all, the smell was irresistible. He inspected beneath the bag as he withdrew it; he knew most knights saddlebags were filled with survival items in case of prolonged journeys.

Alekos sighed in relief as he found fireferns and a candle. After refastening the saddlebag, he turned back towards his old hermitage. He paced towards the house and chuckled when he saw the Elrin peeking gently around the doorway at Alekos. As Alekos neared, however, the creature quickly vacated the entrance.

Alekos entered and immediately the Elrin's face lit from the savoring smell of Loin's meat. However, his face was perplexed, as if he was unfamiliar with who made it. Alekos withdrew a steak and handed it towards the boy who finally seemed to let go of its right shoulder.

The Elrin took it quickly and hastily began to ingest it, and Alekos was torn between smiling at the satisfaction and pitying the poor creature's misery. Though he chose not to decide and instead set the hermitage for camp. He turned to the table which patiently waited for his return.

Noticing the trickle of sunlight evacuating the cabin, Alekos' gaze set upon the dusty candle holder sitting in the middle of the table. He edged closer and let out a sigh as he leaned down to impale the holder's stake through the candle's bottom. Afterward, he straightened the wick and placed the fireferns on the table.

Alekos looked back to the creature, who still ate desperately, and then picked up one of the fireferns. He folded the fern in half holding onto the crease, and as the opposite ends touched a flame burst to life. He lit the candle and unfolded the fern to kill the flame.

"You don't mind staying here tonight do you," Alekos asked as he turned, but then halted as he gazed at his surroundings. Suddenly the hermitage regained its old life, and across the room, was himself laying on the bed tucked in.

He took a step forward in disbelief but then stopped as the door to his right ruptured open. He grabbed at his hilt but stopped shy when the intruder exposed herself as his mother. Helplessly a tear broke from his eye and his feet melted in place.

He watched as his mother ran over to his child self and woke him abruptly. He knew what was going to happen next, for this nightmare has plagued him throughout the endurance of his life. He watched with drenched eyes as his mother confined him into the compartment and spun around, her eyes frantically surveying the room.

She stepped forward and bent down, reaching her hand towards the ground, and magically a sword materialized beneath her hand. It rose to which she grasped its hilt and faced the door. Though her body trembled, her face was etched stern and her strict eyes narrowed like a feline. Tears flooded her eyes, but her heart was strong; she did not dare to move.

Then as the heartbreaking hollers of men echoed louder into Alekos' ears he broke free from his trance. He turned and withdrew his sword as the door burst open off its hinges, the horror embellished by the thunder that followed. As the dark silhouette mocked his memory once more Alekos let out a cry and raised his sword, rushing towards the door, and then there was nothing.

Suddenly he was standing in the dusty hermitage facing the outside, sword drawn. Alekos looked around quickly, breathing deeply and fighting back the tears. He turned around to notice the Elrin had retreated into the cubby.

Alekos' mind went numb, and his sword dropped from his hand, as he plummeted slowly onto his knees. His eyes were tearful, but he fought them back. His teeth clenched, his mind knotted, and he felt nothing inside but a building fire that slowly consumed his vacant shell.

Chapter 7

"I watched my mother killed in front of me from where you are," Alekos spoke after he finally got a hold of himself, "I waited there all night before running into the woods when I could first see light. I woke by a river later, and my caretaker found me."

Alekos stood and looked at the Elrin, whose face seemed ambivalent. "I'm sorry if I frightened you."

"Why do men want you dead," the creature spoke after studying Alekos to make sure it was safe to come out.

"What?" Alekos questioned eagerly.

"My family… sent here to lure you in," Elrin muttered sadly.

Alekos scanned the past few days through his head, "Wait, family? How can you call them family after what they did to you?" he questioned.

"I still feel. I don't know why they don't feel, but they are still my family," Elrin defended softly. "I did this to myself, I didn't want to hold on while going through the hole."

"I'm so sorry," Alekos responded looking at the mutilated arm, "but who is trying to get me, and what hole?"

"I don't know. I don't know, a man?" Elrin answered disappointed.

Alekos thought of his dreams but repressed it, and instead bent to pick up his sword and sheath it. However, as he stood back up, something caught his eye under the bed that he hadn't noticed before. A long narrow chest?

Alekos approached entranced, it was peculiar he hadn't noticed it before. He edged closer, and the Elrin poked his head out to look with him. On the facing side was a crest, but it was faded and no longer legible.

"Has this been here the entire time?" Alekos asked.

"I am not sure," Elrin responded gently.

Alekos bent down and pulled the chest towards him, eager to find out what was inside. He rubbed his hand along the crest and then along the edges of the box, and was intrigued that there was no dust on it. Here goes, he thought as he undid the clasps that held it shut.

He slid his hands to the corners as he lifted it open slowly. It whined as the candlelight slowly entered the chest before exposing its contents. The insides were embroidered in fine cloth, and the bottom had the imprint of what seemed to be a sword. Could this have been my father's sword?

In its place was a scroll wound in a fine silk ribbon. Alekos immediately grabbed the note and brought it to the table for better light. Impatiently he pulled off the bound and unrolled the small parchment. He sat down as he began to read:

When a legend starts, it too must end
When the broken twine becomes amend.
The time and space have both been torn,
But soon unite, so seek the north.
M.S.

"M.S.?" Alekos repeated aloud. The initials bore no meaning to him. He reread the paper and then turned it around. He was confused to see one more phrase. "The Covenant awaits," Alekos spoke as he put the paper down on the table.

Alekos opened his mouth to speak but turned around to see Elrin had already passed out in the cubby. He smiled and stood, pacing over to his old cot. "It seems tomorrow things might finally start to unravel," Alekos spoke softly to himself, "I am unsure whether I should be eager."

He pulled the dusty blanket off the bed that once was his and carried it to the open doorway. He flicked it into the darkness while squinting up to avoid the dirt. As he opened them up he fixated them on the stars. "For you Mother," he spoke softly before snapping his head towards the woods. Something had moved in the trees.

Alekos stared carefully in the direction of the sound, and was met by a glare of a single pair of turquoise eyes. He carefully studied them, not daring to take his eyes off them. However, he relaxed as it turned and ran off into the wilderness.

He shook the blanket once more and then returned into the hermitage, throwing the cover back onto the bed and then lifting the door to cover the threshold. He then went to the table and blew out the candle before blindly making his way to his old cot.

Alekos' body was sore from the long day, and lazily he stumbled onto the bed. He twisted his back popping a few joints before comfortably positioning himself beneath the blanket soundly. Though exhausted his mind still dwelled on things that came and things to come. Though it didn't stop him from passing out moments later.

The next day when he woke the sun was already blaring; he had slept in. He tossed the blanket off of him and jumped from the bed. The table bounced as the Elrin beneath it startled harshly.

"Good morning," Alekos chuckled as he noticed that the boy was eating Loin's meat, "Did you save some for me?"

The young arachne nodded his head as he lifted the bag towards Alekos, and continued to chew the meat that dangled from his lips. Alekos gently took the bag and reached inside, and his stomach growled as he removed the last piece of meat. He smiled as he threw the bag onto the table and took a bite out of the leg of roasted meat.

"We have to leave soon," Alekos spoke tenderly, "it's already late."

He peered out the window, but as he took another bite he heard hoof steps approaching. "Damn it," he murmured frustratingly as he dropped the jerky.

Alekos backed up the volume of the voices raised and turned to the creature. The Elrin must have seen it coming before he did because he was already inside the compartment. Alekos rushed over to him, "You need to be quiet, can you do that?" he spoke apologetically, "Just stay here and don't come out." He shut the compartment door as he turned towards the threshold of his hermitage.

Alekos then grabbed his slingshot from the bed and pulled out a marble from the bag at his waist. The voices outside hushed as they dismounted, but the dead leaves among the ground exposed their position.

Alekos raised the slingshot and aimed as they stopped outside the door; their whispers raising the suspense in the air as they muted.

Suddenly the door was kicked down and immediately Alekos released the bullet as his gaze met with the knight's that welcomed his aim. The bullet scattered forward and plummeted into the man's chest ricocheting him backward unconscious. Alekos quickly pocketed the slingshot as he simultaneously withdrew his sword.

Two more soldiers immediately retaliated by stepping inside, swords already in hand. Alekos didn't want to kill them but he didn't want to be taken prisoner either. He tightened his grip on the sword and took a deep breath, flooding his stomach with cool air as the man to the left stepped forward; Alekos recognized him immediately.

"Don't do it," Garette spoke softly yet firmly, "you haven't killed anyone yet, you don't have to start now."

"Then let me go. I have no ill intentions towards Crewel, and you should know that. I will soon explain when I know myself what is going on, but I must go," Alekos pleaded resolutely.

"You know we can't let you do that, we have orders. Just stop, turn yourself in and save yourself the consequences of worst to come if you don't. You are outnumbered," Garette continued not relaxing his stance.

Alekos gritted his teeth, knowing he was right, and his lungs fluttered as his fear numbed his body. There wasn't a chance he would win this fight unless luck truly was on his side. He bit his lip before speaking, "Fine," he gritted.

Alekos lifted both of his hands and bowed to place his sword gently on the ground. Without hesitation the soldiers came to him, taking hold of his shoulders and grabbed his wrists.

"You shouldn't have run," Garette spoke pitifully to Alekos, "it only—.

Suddenly the compartment behind them slammed open as the soldiers hoisted Alekos to his feet. As the two knights turned Elrin had already scuttled halfway towards them. He turned towards the second knight who simultaneously withdrew his sword.

Alekos rammed Garette to break free from his grip but was already too late to intercept Elrin's attack. Elrin vaulted for the assailant and cut viciously into the knight's chest armor. As he landed back onto the ground he took his arm back to swing again, this time towards his shins.

As Elrin's claws attempted the strike, the knight plunged downwards and impaled Elrin's chest with his sword. Painfully Elrin cried aloud as the cold hard iron pierced his heart and his eyes averted to Alekos'. The air became still as the forest muted.

Alekos' chest caved in as he stared horrified at Elrin's quivering pupils. Slowly the glimmer of light that reflected inside the boy's eye faded as his soul vacated its cavity, and a tear shed from his eye.

Alekos cried out in agony and anger as the young arachne's body crippled slowly, and without thinking, he scooped over the cutthroat. Feverishly he swung down at the pinned man, his fist colliding violently with the man's jaw. Alekos raised his arm once more to swing before his vision went white and he felt his conscience slipping.

The sound of gravel masticating beneath spoked wheels and a pulsating, pinching throb at the back of his head slowly resuscitated Alekos from his unconsciousness. As his vision accommodated to the details around him he felt the stinging burn from rope tightly wound around his wrists and ankles.

He groaned as he turned to see his abductors and the now rehabilitated third knight. Each was conversing with another, but only moments later did Garette turn and notice Alekos being cognizant.

"You shouldn't look so glum," Garette spoke, "if we hadn't found that cart you'd be getting dragged." His sarcastic and humorously cruel tone illuminated his loss of respect for Alekos, but Alekos could have cared less.

He turned his head away and drifted his vision towards the sky; he couldn't help but ruminate on all the bad spirits that have been dwelling around his life mocking it and causing misery. He closed his eyes painfully as the emptiness in his chest plagued his throat and contaminated his mind.

He tried to keep his mind from thinking of the Elrin's despicable fate, but it was futile. Constantly, like a jester who riddled the same riddles, the images of the hard steel piercing the chest of his comrade echoed inside his head. Alekos opened his eyes hoping to draw his attention on his surroundings to prevent himself from continuing to dwell in this misery.

However, ruckus is what caught his attention first. Up ahead of them, horses could be heard neighing, and among them hostile clamor. The knight's halted and dismounted, withdrawing their weapons.

"Cut me loose," Alekos demanded Garette, who only shrugged him off.

Alekos turned to his wrists and began to tug at the ropes with his teeth. As his peripherals exposed the sinister figures he loosened the first knot and then twisted his wrists free. He turned to see the familiar dark soldiers from before coming right at them. A man in the rear raised his arm to draw back an arrow, and as he released the whistle of the arrow skidded past Alekos' face. That happens too much!

As the knights cried out in a charge Alekos turned to focus on untying his ankles. Quickly he kicked off the rope and bounced from the cart. He immediately spotted his weapons sheathed inside the pack strapped to Garette's horse.

He swiftly stooped behind Garette's horse and pulled his

things out just in time to step aside from the rear kick of the horse. Luckily the turmoil that startled the horse kept the knights too busy to notice his escape.

The fight was beginning to become more intense as it seemed an endless horde of black soldiers flooded into the chaos. Alekos withdrew his slingshot and stumbled for a clear shot.

As his gaze fumbled among the tyranny the knight that killed Elrin let out a cry; his knee had been sliced open and another enemy raised his sword to cut him down. Alekos released his grip on the pocket and the ball whistled towards the savage. However, it met a second too late as the brute's sword gashed the knight's throat clean open and blood pulsated across the assailant's arm. A moment later the orb collided with its target, and the foe eradicated.

Alekos shoveled the pouch for another orb and loaded one by one as he sailed them towards the monsters, setting some aflame and others exploding. It seemed nearly too easy until men roared from the forest on all sides; they were surrounded. Alekos released the last two balls towards the two closest to him, sending them spiraling into the distance.

He then abandoned the slingshot, throwing it beneath the cart, and withdrew his sword and turned to focus on the men charging him. Immediately his heart began to beat louder than the pounding footsteps that filled the atmosphere around them.

Alekos charged towards them, unwilling to relinquish his life just yet, and began to step fancily cutting his foes down one by one. His eyes averted from one to another, and his sword clashed expertly against theirs. However, they kept coming as though they were sprouting from the ground, and slowly Alekos began to lose his foothold. He slashed at ankles, calves, arms, and backs, straining to take advantage of every opportunity.

Suddenly another cry was let out and Alekos turned to see that he was alone; the knights had been slain. He scattered his eyes around him timidly, counting ten, twenty, thirty foes. His heart sank and his throat closed choking him; he knew his fate was soon imminent. He tightened his grip on his sword, his eyes blurred in tears, and he began to fight effortlessly and aggressively to prevent what seemed inevitable.

One by one they circled him as the violence reverberated

throughout the air around them. Then suddenly Alekos let out a cry in agony as a sword pierced mercilessly through his calf. He fell to the ground and closed his eyes tightly in pain, a tear breaking from between his clasped eyelids; he knew this was it.

Then there was a thud, and then another, but his fate never came. He opened his eyes, his vision blurred from tears and pain, and all around him he could see the dark figures collapsing. He tried to keep his head up, but, with each pounding beat of his heart, he slowly felt his body draining. His eyes began to cave in as his exhaustion collided with his reality.

Chapter 8

Kojax roared as he hit the now unrecognizable face of the oracle.

"Someone intervened after he was struck down! Half the group you sent never even made it to the site!" the man burst back in retaliation.

Kojax raised his arm to swing once more, but stopped midair and started to chuckle. "I have other plans for them," Kojax hissed as he glared with a crooked smile beneath the shade.

Alekos hurdled from his slumber, uprooting his back from the ground. However, it was a weak attempt for his head weighed heavily on him, and his vision still mocked him with blurs. He stumbled trying to catch his equilibrium, but sudden nausea lashed at him from within his stomach.

"Slow down buddy, you're still hurt. Though I must say it's remarkable how fast you've healed already," said the sound of a soft, but mature, voice, "You'll still need to see a surgeon before you'll be able to walk properly again.".

Alekos stilled himself and closed his eyes. "Where am I?" he asked.

"Safe, and far from those creatures," the male voice replied, "Though there's no time for small talk. You need to eat and build your strength so you can make it to the proper medical attention that you need. There's no doubt you're weak."

Alekos opened his eyes and could make out a wooden bowl being handed to him, and a fire that speckled further off where the meal was prepared. "Thank you," he replied as he weakly took the bowl. "I'm sorry, but what do you mean by creatures," Alekos then asked in confusion. Surely the people they were fighting were human.

"You didn't assume those black-armored humanoids were mundane, did you? Their blood was half coagulated and almost nearly aubergine. That color alone insinuates that they were not human, nor alive for that matter."

"I never noticed the blood, too much chaos for me to focus. You're saying that those were undead monsters that attacked?" Alekos replied, now trying to recall seeing their blood. "More like mutated dead people, now will you eat?" the man said continuing with his demand.

Alekos then turned to look at the bowl after his stomach growled in retaliation to the delay of food entering it. "What is this?"

"Ground hare in a peppergrass seasoned water; trust me it's healthy," the gentleman retorted reassuringly.

"Ground hare? Those things don't come to the surface, and they're impossible to catch. I've never even seen one myself, how did you—

"Just eat," the guy chuckled, "by the way, I'm Darc."

Alekos had already started to drink the soup when Darc spoke his name, so he quickly swallowed before replying. "Thank you for saving my life Darc," he responded before grabbing the first piece of meat and taking a bite. "I'm Alekos," he mumbled through a full mouth, "this is del—."

"Alekos!?" Darc cut in astounded.

"Yes?" Alekos answered with a peculiar look on his face.

"We have to go. Hurry up and finish, I'll pack everything up," Darc said hurriedly, "Don't worry I grabbed your weapons and they're packed safe on the horse for you."

"Wait, what's going on!?" Alekos burst attempting to stand up, but the pain in his calf brought him back down.

"Please, finish eating. I promise I'll explain it on the way, but it's important we get your leg fixed immediately," Darc retaliated sternly.

Alekos opened his mouth to speak but hushed and gritted his teeth. He couldn't stand being clueless about everything that's been happening lately when everyone else, even strangers, seemed to know what was going on and that he was involved. However, he began to scarf the hare as instructed.

He turned to look at Darc who was strapping everything to what seemed to be Garette's horse. Darc then began to rummage through a bag strapped on the other horse, before pulling out a vial. After closing the bag, and refastening it to the horse, he made his way back to Alekos.

"This might burn a little, but honestly I have no idea," he spoke clueless as he reached to undo Alekos' bandages.

"What is it!?" Alekos stammered, pulling his leg back.

Darc grabbed Alekos' ankle and pulled it back towards him, "Kitsune tears, I was given this in my journey to find you. Rare stuff right here," he smirked as he unwrapped the cloth.

Unprepared Alekos sat quietly as Darc opened the vial and poured the fluid over both the entrance and exit wound. Steam rose as Alekos' dry blood sizzled and a small singe burrowed into Alekos' nerves. Then magically the wounds began to slowly disappear, and the pain began to dissipate. Concurrently his vision cleared, as though the wound itself is what made him unable to see.

He looked at Darc and could see that he was only a few years younger than he was. His hair was black and stretched long over his face, and his clothes matched it perfectly. He resembled the image of a hired assassin, with the pale skin and small bladed weapons tucked all over his uniform.

"The tears should have taken the poison out of your system by now. How is your vision?"

"Clear again, thanks," Alekos confounded appreciatively,

shocked in the magic.

"Well, what are you waiting for, test it out," Darc proposed as he stood and reached his hand out to help Alekos up. Alekos took a hold of the outstretched hand and hoisted himself up. His leg felt good as new. He chuckled nervously and hopped on his once injured leg.

"It feels great," Alekos stammered happily, "Thank you!"

"Of course, though you should thank the fox that shed those tears. However, we need to get going if we're going to make it to the Covenant before the sun rises," Darc proclaimed smacking Alekos on the shoulder almost knocking him off balance while turning towards the horses.

Alekos quickly stepped after Darc and got beside him. "What is this Covenant, and how do you know I have to go there. What is going on?" Darc looked at Alekos with a smile and paused for a second next to the horse, "It's a long story. Hop on the other horse; I'll explain it on the way," he answered.

After a few hours, the night grew still, and only the claps of the horseshoes broke the silence of the night. Darc had explained to Alekos about the two brothers who journeyed for the answer behind magical creatures. He told him about the fight, and how everything strange that's been happening lately was because the other brother was trapped in a realm that will eventually tie back to this world.

He explained further that Alekos is the one that is supposed to end it all, and that the great magician had built the Covenant in preparation for his arrival. Of course, Alekos argued that there was no way he could be the one, but Darc reassured him that everything will make sense when they get to the Covenant.

So they rode with the tranquility of the night, as Alekos let everything sink in. How does he fit into this picture? Why is he the one the legend speaks of, and how did everyone know to come after him? He continued to ponder on countless questions, but each argument resulted in the same as his discussion with Darc. It will all make sense when they get to the Covenant.

"How did you fend off all those enemies," Alekos questioned, finally breaking the silence.

Darc looked at him, and his gaze suggested that he was fumbling for the right words. "We live in a world full of wonders and surprises, magic and monsters, yet everyone alive is cursed with being mundane as the water. No special attributes, and no magical source," Darc started, "however there is a lot of this world that can't be explained."

Darc paused for a second and then looked over at Alekos, "Over the years magic has polluted among the mundane, and eventually a tide will rise to a new age. An age of magic," he continued. "We can't control how fate decides our lives to be fit," he stated.

"What are you trying to say," Alekos pondered.

"My mother and father decided living closer to the mountains would make for a suitable home to raise the family. After hundreds of years, the monsters of the mountains become folklore, no matter how many fairies we see. One night phantoms came down from the mountain, attracted to the light that filled their night sky. One of them entered my mother's body, while I was incarcerated in her womb, and possessed her" Darc began, pausing slightly before continuing, "They aren't physical, so they can't kill; they can only pollute and terrorize, or live their life in the shadows."

Alekos stared sentimentally over at Darc, who blatantly was in another world. Darc shook his head and came back to reality before continuing, "My mother went crazy and killed my father, and then abandoned the home to live in the mountains.

"When I was born, the demon left my mother and let her weak and immobile. She was mutilated, and I grew up in the shadows, never feeling hunger nor pain; a part of the physical world with a mortal soul, but not living at all. That's my fate. It wasn't till I met the great wizard that I changed my life around for the better," Darc finished.

"You're saying you're not human?" Alekos asked in confusion.

"I'm saying there are a lot of things in this world that we can't describe. I'm as mortal as you are, just with a few differences," Darc answered.

"Then why is someone like me destined for something so big, when I can't even begin to stand up to forces the magnitude you can," Alekos continued to question.

"Maybe there's more to you than either of us can understand," Darc retaliated with a chuckle, "we'll be there soon so hopefully you'll get the answers you've been waiting for."

By this time they were riding along the bank of a river, ahead rushing water could be heard. "Around this bend, the rapids start to pick up, a waterfall isn't much further down. That's where the Covenant is," Darc stated.

"It can't be, I know these waters. I've been to these falls. There is no town or homes or anything around," Alekos argued.

"Of course you've never seen it, the entrance is behind the first waterfall and it goes underground. The village was built into the cliff wall behind the second waterfall on the oceanfront. So the only way in is by scaling the ocean side, or going down the tunnel hidden by this upcoming waterfall," Darc chuckled.

"It's very complex; I can barely describe it myself, but we'll be there soon so you'll see for yourself what I mean," Darc finished.

Moments later they reached the currents and diverted along the path that descended towards the base of their destination. The waterfall waited, cascading blissfully into a large crystal blue lagoon that extended and flowed towards the ocean beyond. It was there that they forded the water closest to the falls.

Darc directed his horse towards the wall beside the fall. Alekos saw no path but shifted to follow. Suddenly Darc's horse began to rise out of the water in the mist that was birthed by the crashing water. As soon as Alekos' horse began to rise he could see that there were rocks piled beneath the mist, leading up the cliff wall. It was a sharp incline, but as they came out the mist they were on the wall. The horses climbed like goats from each stone, but after they were halfway up the waterfall, there was a tight ledge against the wall. Alekos looked down, and couldn't believe the horses had just scaled what seemed to be a flat cliff wall.

"The founder forged this route so steep so that swimmers wouldn't see the entrance if they swam under the water," Darc informed Alekos as they reached the height of the route. "Watch your head."

Alekos looked ahead to notice a hallway built behind the

waterfall. The roof extended further out than the path so that if anyone looked up from below the illusion would be that the wall was concave and curved at the top.

As soon as they were behind the rushing water a pitch-black threshold met them. Darc motioned forward, and immediately the darkness swallowed them. The reigns of Alekos' horse were pulled, and they came to a stop. "If it was during the day you'd be able to see better, but I don't have a torch so you're going to have to trust me," Darc warned Alekos as he reached his hands towards Alekos' face.

"What," Alekos began as Darc's hands reached his brows, but then suddenly the cavern lit up in a black and white infrared view. "What did you do to me?" Alekos stammered nervously.

"I put shadows in your eyes," Darc answered, "your eyes can't capture light in the darkness, so I made them capture darkness like mine does. In other words, you can see in the dark now. Don't worry, it's not permanent."

Darc chuckled as he beckoned the horse forward without waiting for Alekos to reply. Astounded Alekos followed, looking at everything around him. The tunnel began to bend and descend, and, eventually, Alekos could tell they were underneath the waterfall.

The pounding whistle of the water roared overhead as the two riders crept deeper into the cave. He could see water trickling from holes in the ceiling into dugout waterways that resembled aqueducts. The water then flowed along both sides of the tunnel towards the direction they were heading.

Slowly the deafening sound of the water hushed in the distance, and a light could be seen flickering in the distance. The noise of civilization could be heard resonating off the rocky walls. "Welcome to the Covenant," Darc exclaimed, breaking the silence.

At the end of the tunnel, the cave opened up and ahead stood the village of the Covenant. Torches lit up the town, but the light seemed magically confined inside the village since none bounced against the cavern walls. At the opposite end of the cave, Alekos could see the large opening, smothered from pouring water from the river above them. The ocean could be heard just beyond it, as the water plummeted down into its belly.

Suddenly color returned to Alekos' sight as Darc reached over and placed his hand on Alekos' head once more, and the beauty of the Covenant flooded his vision. A mystical forest smothered the ceiling above the village, and faeries light could be seen as they flew around in their upside-down world.

The streams of water channels bowled around the great circular cavern, and the roots could be seen stretching for them. Even more so bewitching, on either side of the path that led to town, growing up towards the aqueducts, rainbow pyrite and quartz garnished the landscape.

"This is remarkable," Alekos breathed astonished.

"Well none of this would be possible without magic," Darc retorted humorously, "The founder began building it about a decade and a half ago, and didn't finish for eight years."

Fifteen years ago, Alekos thought to himself, that was when my mother was killed. Alekos began to flashback before being interrupted by the clapping of horseshoes coming their way.

It was a younger guy than Darc with long blonde hair, and seemingly glowing skin, riding on the back of a black stallion. "Xarth!" Darc burst excitedly as he rode his horse over to meet him. Alekos waited as the two conversed inaudibly, but after a few seconds, Alekos was motioned to approach.

"It's good to finally meet you," Xarth said, putting his hand out in greeting, "I know this might come as a shock to you, but your name has quite a story to it."

"So I've heard," Alekos replied shaking his hand in return but flinched as static intervened the clasp.

"Haha, forgive me. You'll have to get used to that with me," Xarth chuckled.

Chapter 9

As Xarth led them towards the village, Alekos could see that another path parted within the glistening stone scenery. It appeared to have gone to a clearing near another dark tunnel. As soon as they entered the village, the vacant streets became garnished with whispers that came from the windows on each side. They continued past the first sets of buildings and into another clearing. Across the courtyard was a large building that Alekos assumed was their point of destination.

Outside the building stood a very large man, with a head too small for his torso. His nose was pressed in, and his hair was high and tight, bald on the sides and trimmed expertly on top.

Xarth went to him first and asserted that they needed to see the wizard. "It's Alekos," he pointed out when the grunt averted his eyes to the stranger. Immediately the stern hard face of the human boulder relaxed in inquiry, "Are you sure?" his voice boomed.

Xarth turned to look at Darc, who looked at Alekos, then concurrently they nodded their heads. The man turned and went up the steps into the door of the building, and Xarth directed the group around the side.

There they approached a hitching rail where the three dismounted and proceeded in tying their horses. After finishing they returned together to the face of the building.

By then the large man had returned outside, "He is ready," he rumbled as he opened the door, "Darc, Xarth, stay out here." The two immediately obeyed him and turned away, but Alekos continued up the steps and towards the door.

The sound of the heavy door clasping together behind him vibrated his chest and immediately his nerves began to rattle. He gazed around, studying the hall before him. It was grand and vast much like Crewel's dining hall. Although there were no long tables, and steps leading up to a throne, there were giant carved beasts that adorned the giant room. Above him, the roof appeared transparent, and the forest above him resembled that of a starry sky.

One beast caught his eye at the rear of the room. It was a giant spider, and looked in every way like the creatures he had encountered except without the human torso. It was just one giant, disturbing spider. Suddenly a door closing at the front of the hall snatched Alekos' attention from the beast. He turned to see the back of the man who closed the door. Like a king, the man was adorned with majestically polished armor that stood out from behind the tattered cloak he bore.

"Alekos," he said immediately before turning, "I see you found interest in our library, that happens to be an Arachne," He lectured as he began to make his way across the hall.

"I've heard that before, but the beast it was referring to had a torso like a centaur. I want to know what the hell is going on." Alekos sternly interjected, his patience wearing greater than his nerves.

The man slowed his step as he neared Alekos, and let out a sigh. "Yes, I do believe you deserve an explanation." He motioned his arm for Alekos to sit on one of the many benches that waited in front of each statue. "Please sit."

Alekos paused for a second before joining the man for a seat, yet still, his frustration boiled inside of him. The man turned to look at Alekos, his face curled as he fumbled for words.

"You must be wondering about these monstrous creatures that are spilling into the forest, why the weather is getting worse, and why it all focuses on you," the man stated.

"No Darc did most the pleasure of telling about the pitiful family feud and that I'm supposed to end it, but what I don't understand is why me," Alekos responded assertively.

"Alekos listen to me, and know that everything I tell you won't be easy to hear," the man started before pausing. "My name is Megahte, I'm the wizard who sent my brother into a replica realm of this world. I'm also your father--"

"What!?" Alekos burst as he jumped from the bench, "The hell are you talking about, my parents are dead!"

"Calm down," Megahte hushed as he grabbed for Alekos' hand.

"No! Tell me what the hell you're talking about," Alekos retaliated back snatching his hand from Megahte's reach.

Megahte rose from the bench and turned towards Alekos'. "Fifteen years ago, my brother, your uncle, attacked me from behind like a coward, full of hatred for my powers. I fought him, but I couldn't kill the brother I grew up protecting my whole life."

"So you decide to throw it on me, telling me you're my father like you expect me to pity you?" Alekos stammered gritting his teeth as his anger fueled inside him.

"You can't change fate Alekos, I'm incapable of finishing the job because I was just not fast enough sending him to another realm," Megahte said raising his voice while unstrapping his chest plate. He laid it on the bench, before pulling his tunic's collar down to expose his chest. "He brought my guard down, telling me even if I kill him there, my wife and son will still be dead before I get home."

Alekos' gaze drifted up from the scar across Megahte's chest towards his sorrowful eyes. "I thought you were dead, but the prophecy of an oracle spoke of your survival and how you will rise in power to fix what I can't do myself. I'm so sorry I couldn't find you sooner," Megahte said softly as he fell back onto the bench.

"I've been using my power to get ready for the great battle, building this Covenant, hoping you were alive, yet preparing for a battle if otherwise. You have no idea how happy I am to finally see you again," Megahte continued.

Alekos stood quiet, conflicted on the words he was

hearing, could everything he is hearing be true?

"Look," Megahte said, as he withdrew the sword on his waist. Concurrently as it was unsheathed Alekos drew back as his heart sunk.

"That's the sword my mother used to try to fight off the intruders," Alekos breathed shaken.

"It's my sword, I left it with her while I was out. I found it… when I returned home. There was no sign of you, and I thought the worse," Megahte stated, trying to convince Alekos of his words.

Then Alekos too sunk onto the bench, his heart too heavy to allow him to stand. "It all makes sense now," Alekos murmured through the pain.

"I'm sorry it had to be this way, fate is a strong foe to get around." Megahte expressed, "I'll leave you be if needed, for you to take time, but when you're ready, there's food. You'll need it if you expect to train. There are only three days until the realms align, but I will not push you if you are not ready."

"I'm ready," Alekos gritted sternly, "Don't think I'm doing this for you though. That bastard killed my mom, tried to kill me, and I'm going to make him regret that decision."

The door opposite of the one Megahte entered was designated to be Alekos' quarters. Megahte left him in the room to begin preparations for the village breakfast, allowing Alekos to get the solitude he unknowingly needed.

He sat down, took a few breaths, and then laughed out loud as he realized how crazy he was. He always wanted something more in life, but every opportunity he ran from to enjoy his tranquility. The quiet, vacant room soothed him, but it wasn't long before he got antsy much like he always would.

Alekos retreated to the hall, hoping to find a sense of belonging, and immediately halted upon his exit. To his surprise, a giant stone beast was walking around the courtyard changing the ground with the stomp of his feet. It leaned over and tapped the group with the tip of its finger and a fountain elegantly blossomed in response.

Frozen in shock, Alekos watched as stone stools and tables began to rise from the ground. Though, shortly after, the giant turned to exit the courtyard through an alley as he appeared to have finished. His footsteps shook the ground with each step, and as the shaking lightened Alekos knew it was gone.

Shortly after his trance was broken when a hand slapped his shoulder and gripped a hold. It was Darc. "So how did the meeting with the great wizard go?"

"According to him, he's my father," Alekos replied coming back to reality. "Did not see that coming."

"Yeah, sorry I didn't tell you that part. Didn't think you'd take the journey if I did," Darc laughed.

"I understand, I probably would have thought you were crazy."

It wasn't long before their teasing conversation was joined by much more audible clamor. It seemed as though the villagers were retired from their homes to the courtyard. Darc led Alekos to one of the tables, and each claimed a spot before there were none left. Of course, the beast had made enough for everyone.

Three others joined their table, Xarth among them. Another was a boy who shared the same color hair as Alekos, his eyes, however, were bright orange. He couldn't be much older than Elrin. The other was also young. She had hair was so thick it came down like vines. Her hair was blonde, with the occasional green strands encircling her dreads, which accented her emerald eyes flawlessly.

It turned out that the boy's name was Pyrus and the girl's Vyne. They also had been rescued by Megahte and spoke highly of him. Alekos was surprised to hear that they both were found when they were old enough to barely walk. However, before he could ask about that the air was immediately filled with a sweetness that drew his attention. He looked up to see the faeries plucking fruit that ripening in seconds, and flying them down the center of the tables.

Excitement crossed the tables, as they received their breakfast. Alekos gazed in awe at the wonderful sight of magic and man living in harmony. Few creatures dared to live with or even near humans. Suddenly he was nudged by Darc.

"I got a surprise for you," Darc stated as he pulled out a bag from beneath the table, "I found this in the knight's rucksack."

It was the bag of Loin's meat!

"I have the hare, but I figured you're more adjusted to this. It's okay, most here are used to me eating meat."

Alekos' face lit with glee as he received the bag. "Thank you so much!" He looked inside to see a couple of strips and a leg left. "So almost everyone here refrains from meat?" he asked as he pulled out the leg and folded the bag.

"Pretty much, some don't eat at all. Like me for example, I don't need to eat to live. I just do it for the sport, and to feel alive." Darc joked.

It was just then that Alekos' attention was stolen. Across the room was this young woman, looking right at him. She was the only one there that looked his age besides Darc and Vrachos. Her hair was long and silky and covered most of her face, but there was no mistake that she was looking at him.

"Who is that?" He asked Darc, as he studied every detail.

"To be honest I don't know. Sometimes she's here, and other times she's not. Megahte would know though, she only ever talks to him."

Alekos made no response and continued to share his gaze as he finished his leg. He reached forward for a plum to wash down the meat, and as he looked back up the lady was gone. He looked around to no avail, and decided to finish his meal. Afterward, he told Darc he was going for a walk.

He first went to his horse to put away his strips in the sack, before going to the opening that led to the ocean. The rushing water of the river that flowed into the ocean below drowned his hearing and soon he was in his own world, gazing peacefully through the wall of water. However, it wasn't long before his solitude was interrupted.

"Alekos?" said a soft female voice from behind.

The surprise caused him to flinch and, after nearly slipping, he hopped from back from the edge of the cliff. "That's my name," he replied innocently hiding his shock. He turned to look at the lady, who wore a dark brown tunic with white lace borders. There was a slit that finished the female attire exposing the top of her plump breasts, but he quickly averted his eyes to her gaze.

"Umm," choked Alekos, "Yes, that's my name." He chuckled disguising his flushed face is humor. "Have we met before," he added after noticing she was the one that was staring at him.

"If I am correct, I believe just now," she giggled, "My name is Azalea. It's nice to meet you,"

Alekos smiled and took her outstretched hand to shake, "Likewise, and I'm relieved to not get shocked," he chuckled as his hand met hers.

"Haha no, Xarth is the first thunder nymph to exist," Azalea smiled back shaking his hand.

"You'll have to forgive me for asking, but he's what exactly?"

"Everyone here was born as a result of a magical origin. Xarth was born on the other side of the mountains by a bolt of lightning, or so Megahte says. He was born naturally with a connection to the static realm," she explained shyly.

"Darc told me about the ruins on the other side of the mountains where the fight took place. I can assume then that Xarth was his first encounter with your kind?" Alekos inquired curiously.

"My kind? That's a little discriminating. What makes you think I'm like anyone here?"

"I'm sorry, I didn't mean to offend. I just meant that everyone here is different than me. Not in a bad way, or anything. I just… I don't know, this is different for me. I guess I'm just curious as to why you're here."

"If I told you, I'd have to kill you," she teased Alekos before finally smiling.

"That wouldn't be smart, apparently I'm supposed to hinder a supposed doomsday," Alekos jokingly responded. Azalea chuckled and kicked at the ground shyly before looking up just beyond Alekos.

"I see you met Azalea. Careful she's rambunctious," laughed Megahte as Alekos turned around, "I'm glad you joined the town for breakfast. If you're serious in committing to this journey you'll need your strength."

"Well like you said, we have three days. I'm ready to start this when you are," Alekos answered.

"Okay," Megahte nodded quickly before turning, "Follow me."

"It was nice to meet..," Alekos started as he turned to say goodbye to Azalea, but she was already gone.

"... You," he finished as he turned to follow Megahte.

"This place is full of voids," Megahte began as Alekos caught up to him, "Magical barriers that blind the mundane of this places existence, and helps to keep the light and smoke from exposing our haven to the outside world. Eight years it took me to perfect the beauty and science that constructed this mesopotamia for the mystical living. Every time I harvest magic it harvests life from me, and my heart has become weaker with time."

"When you say it, you're talking about the medallion?" Alekos asked.

"Yes, and if you are serious in taking this journey you will need it. I won't live long without it, because its magic is what's keeping my heart alive, but inevitably it is yours as part of my will to you.

"This medallion contains so much mystery, and I hope, when this journey comes to an end, you can continue the quest I started," he finished as they reached a clearing not too far from the village.

As they approached, thundering footsteps could be heard again and the giant from earlier came into sight.

"Right on time Vrachos," Megahte said as the big man halted with a thud, "how's the boy doing?"

Suddenly the stone giant began to crumble, and in the rubble stood Vrachos. "He is healing. Doctor is still with him. It is the poison," Vrachos boomed in response. It was obvious he was attempting to whisper, but his form prevented him from doing so.

"What boy?" Alekos asked joining Megahte and Vrachos.

"Shortly before you arrived, a scout found a tree nymph dying in the woods," Megahte answered, "Being part of the Covenant's core, we strive to ensure the safety and survival of all magic nature. Everyone here is a result of my preservation of magic."

"Safety and survival, peace and serenity, you sound like Crewel," Alekos replied.

"I don't think Crewel has a passion for life as we do," another voice chuckled from behind them. It was Darc, who seemed to come from nowhere.

"You've always had a knack for a surprise entrance," Megahte smiled.

"I just came to enjoy the show," Darc joked back, "which doesn't seem like is going to happen with all this yapping."

"We're just waiting on—" Suddenly a yellow flash interrupted him, "Never mind."

"Sorry I'm late, I was doing rounds after we discovered the boy to make sure no one followed us," Xarth huffed, catching his breath.

"No it's fine, we just arrived," Megahte pardoned Xarth as he stepped up to them.

"Am I fighting him unarmed?"

"No," Megahte answered before turning to see Alekos bare of his weapons. "Where is your sword?"

"Shit, I wasn't thinking," Alekos stammered, "they're still on my horse."

"I got it!" Darc exclaimed before dropping into the ground.

Alekos flinched, finally seeing Darc's ability. "That is so cool."

"Shadows cover this world, and each one is a window for him to travel through. It is very important to be educated in the magic of this world. Especially if your opponent is supernatural. The great library was built for this purpose."

Then immediately Darc reappeared in front of them holding Alekos' sword. He outstretched his arm to hand it over, and as soon as Alekos' hand gripped the hilt Darc's eyes averted as he vanished.

Alekos spun as he heard quick steps behind him and saw Xarth coming at him. He stood his ground as Xarth slid a hand across his forearm materializing a lightning blade. Alarmed, Alekos stepped back as Xarth raised the electric sword to swing down on him.

Alekos raised his sword smacking the blade of lighting

which then disintegrated. Then suddenly Xarth's other hand collided with the side of Alekos' face, and a foot met the back of his knee, collapsing him. Fuck, he's fast.

Xarth then created another to swing at Alekos, who turned just in time to instinctively fall backward and barely dodge his assailant's sword that too decomposed after being swung.

"Are you trying to kill me," Alekos sputtered stumbling back trying to get on his feet.

"How else will you learn to not be killed by those trying to kill you," Megahte exclaimed as Xarth flicked his fingers towards Alekos.

A miniature bolt flew from each hand; the first skid past Alekos as he stood, and the other Alekos expertly chopped out the air moments before it collided with his chest. He then turned to charge his opponent who already had another sword made. He knew the weak point now in his attacker's offense.

He ducked low and scooped up some rocks in his gallop and hurled them at Xarth. As Xarth raised his guard, the sword vanished and Alekos was already there. With his grip tight on his sword, Alekos grilled Xarth in the jaw with his knuckles, sending him to his knees.

"Excellent," Megahte called out as Xarth hit the ground, "Xarth rarely takes a hit, but if you can keep up with his speed let's test yours."

Alekos turned to see Vrachos turning back into the hulk, as the ground around him attached itself to his body. After reaching his doubled height, he stomped the ground sending a club, which resembled a stalagmite, from the ground to his hands.

"You gotta be kidding me," Alekos breathed in disbelief.

Chapter 10

"The ability to dodge is the most lethal in defeating your opponent," Megahte preached aloud, "unless your opponent is Vrachos and doesn't get tired. Haha"

Alekos gritted his teeth as the human boulder stomped the ground once more and swung his club at the mass of rubble that ascended from the ground. Alekos dove to the side, rolling back onto his feet just as his rival crashed in front of him in a single leap across the clearing. The impact rattled Alekos' knees sending him falling back onto his rear. Fear pumped adrenaline through Alekos' veins as he turned to run, seeing the brute start to swing, and his heart climbed into his throat as the club struck the ground right from where he pushed off.

They really are trying to kill me!

Another rumble went through the ground as soon as he was on his feet, and immediately Alekos turned his head to see Vrachos throwing a large rock. Halfway in a starting sprint, he swung around and tripped backward causing the mass of stone to go spiraling over him.

Suddenly the beast was in front of him in another crashing leap. He raised his club over his head, and then suddenly his head snatched in the direction of the cave village.

"Someone is here," He boomed as he started towards the cave entrance.

Alekos sat up, his heart beating violently in his chest, and noticed everyone else was running after Vrachos. Darc had already vanished. He jumped up and took off, sword in hand.

"Stop!" Darc screamed as he appeared in front of Vrachos, who was nearly at the entrance. "Vrachos cave in the entrance, we need to get everyone out of here now!"

"What's happening," Megahte called out while catching up.

Suddenly a loud thud shook the cavern, and a howl pierced the air and reverberated against the chasm walls. "They're coming in! There's a mutated wendigo trying to bust down the supporting walls of the pool under the falls!" Darc exclaimed.

"Dammit. You and Xarth get everyone out of here, Vrachos and I will give you as much time as we can," Megahte started, "Alekos go with them!"

Instinctively, everyone dashed in their ordered direction, except Alekos who stared at Megahte.

"Vrachos hold them off at the entrance. Cave it in if I'm not back in ten minutes, then go with the rest!" Megahte demanded.

Alekos opened his mouth to speak just in time to see Megahte vanish, so he straightened his focus on his belongings. Darc vaporized in the front and simultaneously an alarm went off in town. Xarth ran so fast he was in the town before Alekos reached halfway.

As soon as he reached the town, another boom vibrated the chasm and chaos could be heard howling through the tunnel. Alekos broke past rushing people, striving to get to his horse, and turned towards the great hall. Once arriving, he stripped the rucksack off and fastened it to himself, then untied the reigns.

After he mounted he directed the horse towards the entrance and kicked to induce his horse's gallop. He charged past citizens, rushing for the roars of the enemies ahead, and could see Vrachos already swinging his club at the black humanoids, killing them instantly in a single blow.

Alekos reached in his self-made backpack for his slingshot, and pulled out an orb from his waist pouch. Expertly he whistled the orb past Vrachos by inches and blasted a ten-foot radius with a fiery explosion as it collided with the upcoming wave of soldiers.

"Keep it up, I'm going to catch up with Megahte!" he hollered as he galloped past Vrachos.

The tunnel, now much brighter in the day, was full of hollers from the approaching danger, but he charged deeper. As he came upon the next wave, he drew back another bullet and sent it directly towards the middle, cutting a path violently through the center of them.

Shortly after brushing past the crowd he could see Megahte ahead in a violent battle; he was fighting both a monster and the soldiers that stopped instead of rushing inwards like the rest.

Alekos had never seen anything like it before. The massive beast resembled a man hunched over, with hair infesting from his head down his back. His face was stretched forward like a canine, bordered with extruding fangs, and his ears were made of bone which resembled that of a stag's antlers. His feet were hoofs, and his hands were like the Arachne only hairy. Even stranger, he had enormous bat wings folded behind his back. Alekos stared in shock at horrendous and magnificent sight..

Megahte was majestic. He was flawless, almost divine-like. First creating a shield of stone over his sword hand to bash the enemies back with his arm, and then spinning and throwing his other arm towards the wendigo beast, blasting a wave of energy through his hand to smack it back against the wall. Then turning back forward he swung his sword arm, the rubble crumbled off the sword, and sliced through an attacking soldier.

Suddenly a spear pierced Alekos' horse's chest, and the horse reared sending Alekos onto his back with his leg pinned beneath the horse.

“Gahhh!” Alekos cried out in pain as he felt his knee pop. He turned to see enemies rushing towards him.

One raised a sword as he dashed to cut down Alekos and suddenly a blast sent him and the others spiraling overhead.

“Get up boy!” Megahte yelled out to Alekos from inside his battle.

“I'm stuck!”

Then instantly the horse listed off his leg as Vrachos appeared out of nowhere. He placed his hands on Alekos' leg and snatched it back in place, filling the tunnel with a curdling scream of agony.

“On your feet,” Vrachos demanded as he yanked Alekos to his feet. Alekos cried out again bracing the pressure, but then a cracking sound was heard that made the entire tunnel hush.

The ceiling began to fracture, it was going to cave in.

“Get him out of here now!” Megahte screamed as a field of energy massed around his body and expanded, trapping all the malicious soldiers and the beast inside.

Vrachos suddenly began to grow as stones encased his body, and Alekos was suddenly yanked off the ground as the giant sprinted towards the covenant.

The ceiling began to cave in behind them and Alekos stared blankly as the light from the mass of energy faded beneath the rubble. However, the cave started swallowing faster, so as they neared the entrance to the covenant, without warning, Vrachos lifted Alekos and threw him as hard as he could.

“No, wait...Fu--,” was all Alekos could burst before the air sucked out from his lungs.

He soared over the town, and under the trees, in an instance, and the next he was beaming towards the wall of rushing water.

“Oh shit,” he gasped before breaking through the water and seeing the two hundred foot drop to the oceanfront. Once more the air was vacuumed out his lungs as he feared an imminent death.

He began to fall when it came to him. That's it, Alekos remembered through the adrenaline. He reached for his side, but then realized his slingshot wasn't there. Everything went quiet in his head as his heart sunk. He couldn’t escape the situation, as he had helped the creature. The calm ocean below quickly revealed its harsh waves as he neared. This was it.

Then out of nowhere, the cliff wall exploded as Vrachos broke out from the wall below and caught Alekos in the air. As they spiraled towards the ocean, Vrachos rolled and placed his back towards the water holding Alekos above him. Seconds later the muffled sound of thunder crashed against his eardrums as they struck the ocean.

"No!" Kojax roared as he marched towards the oracle.

"It was a feeble mission to attack the enemy's home territory," retorted the man who held his head high. "Maybe you should have run that plan by me first."

Kojax scrunched his face in anger and withdrew his sword, piercing the oracle instantly. He then turned to a soldier who was with him, the old man's body swinging off the sword, "Tell me something I want to hear."

"When the day realigns and the realms tie, you'll be able to lead us. Your army won't fail with you in front," the soldier responded quickly.

"Have everyone at the ruins by tomorrow evening. When the void opens fully we'll go through and take back what is rightfully mine!" Kojax turned as lightning bellowed above and walked off

The next thing Alekos felt was the urge to vomit as he exhaustively coughed up the salty liquid within him. He gazed about to see faces, all around him, staring at him. He then turned to the presence of the person beside him. It was Azalea.

She smiled and turned rosy as she stood up. "Thank you," Alekos breathed wiping his mouth, as he turned hot realizing what she had done. She bowed her head but didn't say anything. Then someone else approached him.

"What do we do now?"

It was Darc.

"Why are you asking me?" Alekos replied.

"Megahte's dead," Vrachos rubbled from the crowd, "I can't feel heartbeat through ground."

"You're the next in the bloodline to lead us, the one that's prophesied to save this world," Darc added.

Alekos suddenly drew back to reality. Suddenly hatred consumed his body, his father deserved a burial not caused by a monster.

"We need to go back. Megahte deserves a proper ceremony," Alekos stated while standing, "Then we'll discuss the obliteration of this psychopath."

It was evident Alekos was fueled with fire, and everyone immediately coordinated with a plan of formation. They were close to the other waterfall, but there was no knowing if any danger could still be lurking.

However, the solemn walk went smoothly until they arrived at the nightmare. Nothing but rubble filled the hole that once was the Covenant and its passage. Filled with sorrow they made their way along the river of rubble, watching as water slowly appeared in the rocks as they neared the fall.

"Darc, can you see him?" Alekos asked as they got closer.

"I'm looking," he replied with pitch-black eyes as he scanned the rubble, "There are a lot of bodies."

"I feel the big one through the rocks," Vrachos echoed as he pointed in the direction he mentioned.

"I think he's beneath it," Darc declared after looking as directed.

Vrachos immediately bent over and touched the ground. As his hand rested on the ground the rubble began to twist, shaking the earth beneath their feet. Seconds later, as a gap appeared, a body could be seen limply beneath the strange beast.

Darc vanished then reappeared next to the body and began to drag it up onto the surface of the rubble, and then once more reappeared in front of them, holding Megahte's lifeless body. The sword was still in Megahte's hand, and as his other hand fell off his chest the medallion fell out from inside.

Darc lifted it and handed it to Alekos, who paused before taking it.

"It's yours now, including the sword," Darc stated, "You need to be armed with something other than a bag of bullets without a slingshot."

"Yeah" Alekos murmured as he knelt to take the sword.

He wrapped the medallion around the hilt of the sword, and then stood back up. “Let's not bury him again.”

The others looked at Alekos, and then immediately got to work. Vrachos built a stone shrine at the top of the waterfall, splitting the flow of water around the tunnel entrance that was now a hole to nowhere. He also cleared the rubble so that a river could reform. Xarth scattered about and quickly collected branches, and after only a short while they had built a funeral fit for a king.

As the sun began to set, everyone gathered at the top of the falls, watching as Pyrus volunteered to light the ceremonial fire. He slowly walked up to the altar and reached out as he neared the bed of branches. Then suddenly, as his finger touched, a fire consumed the bed.

Pyrus then remained standing by the bed, in flames. Alekos had become used to the shock of magic nature by then and stood unconcerned.

“His mother was burned alive and left to die in the woods by his father after getting pregnant by a fire nymph. A baby lay crying in the ashes after the fire went out, and Megahte found him,” Darc whispered as he noticed Alekos watching the boy.

“How did Megahte get lucky finding everyone?” Alekos asked as he was brought out his thoughts.

“Beats me, but I choose not to question fate,” Darc replied as he turned to leave.

Chapter 11

Soon after the fire dwindled to nothing but embers flickering within the ashes, and everyone slowly retreated to the campsite that was set up for the night. Alekos was the last to leave, even after Pyrus returned to his mundane state and left to join the company.

As he neared the campsite a beam of moonlight illuminated from behind the clouds casting itself on Alekos. He stopped and looked up. Then he looked down and the medallion was brightly glowing around the hilt of his father's sword.

He unwound it from the sword and lifted it in front of him. The bright gold mystified him, he could feel the power generating from the medallion. He could feel it calling for him.

He pulled it to him and lifted the chain above his head. Then, as he slid it down, he abruptly fell back losing his breath, and everything went white.

Suddenly he found himself surrounded by darkness, a loud ringing echoing all around him. He grabbed his ears as he fought against it on his knees.

"LISTEN TO ME!" bellowed an unknown voice above, beyond the high pitched drumming. "This medallion manipulates the forces of magic, if you are not careful you too can be manipulated!"

The screeching sound of deafness grew louder until it cut out the deep majestic voice, and suddenly Alekos found himself high in the mountains. He tried to stand but a gust of wind knocked him down at the edge of the cliff he was on.

He looked down, and he saw Dead Man's Gorge. The passageway that connected the continent to the unknown beyond. "Many legends were told of the battle that took place through this pass that secured serenity and prosperity on the mainland of Laquaderia," the voice began.

The ringing finally quit, and the sky lit up like a warm summer day. "The mundane made stories that obscured the beauty of life," it continued from the heavens. "Even you are blind to the truth, but this deadly path is a gate to all the answers you need."

Once more there was a ringing and the world around him began to spin before he found himself in the center of a grand colosseum. Grass completely covered the courtyard, and, instead of benches and booths arranged around the arena, giant chairs were constructed evenly into the stone of the infrastructure encircling him. Trees were in the process of sprouting from the ground when instantaneously they halted and shriveled back into the ground. The grass around Alekos' feet began to wither and then he shot into the sky above the arena. Revealing that it was on a piece of land on the other side of the mountains, surrounded by ocean.

"Before you can know about the beginning, you must first stop the end," the voice bellowed hauntingly, as the sky went rapidly from night to day.

Alekos looked below him to see the colosseum slowly turning into lifeless ruins, then suddenly a flash of light burst from the center of the arena. He looked but nothing was there as time seemed to be rapidly flying forward before it skidded to an abrupt stop. Storm clouds crackled above, and the ocean around the peninsula had vanished. In its place was darkness, and the only light came from the ravenous horde of monstrous creatures and demonic soldiers that filled the entire land mass between the arena and the narrow pass that led to the Gorge.

Alekos gaped in fear at the horrendous atmosphere, as the many fires danced to mutiny around. They were everywhere. Some monsters resembled a smaller, more man-like, wendigo beast like they had met earlier. They had horns, some broken and some fine to the point, on their head between the antlers, and a set of open broken ribs sprouting from their hunched back. Their noses seemed like that of a bat's, and their eyes burned a bright orange. Instead of being hairy, they were skeletal, some almost rotten, and they bore no wings.

Suddenly the ringing began again, and all the monsters roared. A small black orb materializes above him, purple sparks violently emitted around it.

Alekos stood staring in fear, as he realized what was going on. The orb began to grow downwards, consuming his body and immediately he went deaf and everything went white again as a burning sensation grew on his skin. He squinted through his pressed eyes to see the arms he was using to cover his ears changing colors. He sucked in a deep breath in shock and his bones started popping in his back. He let out a scream, then suddenly he was shaken back to reality.

He realized he was screaming in the moonlit clearing, and people had come to see what happened. Darc was the one in front of him, still holding Alekos by the shoulders.

Alekos panted as feared painted his soaking wet body.

"What happened," Darc stammered as Alekos' gaze focused on him.

Alekos looked down and picked the medallion up from his chest, "I don't know how, but it showed me. I saw the army. I saw the monsters. I know where they are."

"Okay, we need to get him to the camp," Darc demanded to the others around him as he hoisted Alekos to his feet.

Alekos couldn't steady himself, and his vision doubled constantly, so Darc and another man he didn't know helped him walk back as the others gathered around.

They got back and everyone was in the center gathered in

front of the new fire. By then Alekos was walking on his own, only his head hurt. He shook his head as he got to the gathering.

"Vrachos," he called the largest shadow in front of the fire. "I need Xarth too."

The two came to him and Alekos motioned for Darc to come closer as well.

"They're at Origenesis , I actually saw the ruins. The army is even more massive than I could have thought. Those black soldiers don't even make up a small fraction of the monsters he has." Alekos started, his heart finally slowing down to keep pace with his breath. "We need to be ready, and as much help as we can get."

"What are you saying?" Darc broke in.

"We need to warn the kingdom," Alekos stammered. The others backed away from him, and he staggered keeping his balance. "What?"

"We are a family, and the Covenant is all we've had since we left our lives behind. How could you put our safety at risk to warn people who would see you imprisoned?" questioned Darc amongst the silence.

"It's not about us or them, it's about the prosperity of our land. Kojax has a horde with him, and we will get trampled without everyone conjoining for the same cause," Alekos argued. They all kept quiet before Azalea stepped into the dancing light.

"I'll go with you," she said softly, "I'm the only one who travels near the villages. We can get there faster together"

"This is not what Megahte would have wanted, he would want you doing everything you can do master that medallion!" Darc shouted before vanishing in an instant. Alekos stumbled forward after trying to confront him and Azalea placed herself in Alekos' sight, concurrently putting her hand on his shoulder.

"What did you want to do? We don't need to waste time just because the sun isn't out."

By now most had abandoned the fire, and were going to lie down; they wanted no part of it either. Vrachos was the only one who was still there, but he was probably too dim to see the light of the situation.

"I was thinking about telling the old king since he's the only one who'd probably listen to me without incarceration,"

Alekos began, "but it's unknown where he's retired at."

"Then let's get going."

The sun was just becoming visible on the horizon behind them when they finally reached a path that led towards civilization. Instead of getting on they kept beside it, the whole trip neither spoke a word. Alekos was in his own world anyway. No one knows the origin of life, but there is one truth that was known. Man and magic have lived separately from each other in harmony ever since they came through the mountains. He thought of the legends that spoke of the great beasts in the mountains that hunted down our ancestors.

The library brought those legends to life, and yet he's yet to meet a single one like described. He thought of the mysterious ruins on the peninsula that could reside on the other side of the mountains, and how life could have started there; why all life left there in the first place. How did the medallion show this to him, and could it really be real?

"Hey, you there," Azalea questioned Alekos as she walked beside him.

"I'm sorry, what?" Alekos asked blinking his eyes as if just noticing the sunlight.

"I said we should almost be there," she answered with a forgiving smile.

"I'm really sorry, I've just been through so much."

"Don't worry yourself, I can't imagine the heartbreak you're feeling."

Azalea pulled in Alekos and forced in a hug, but Alekos was already trying to cheer up so he pulled back and looked her in her eyes. He couldn't help but think of the eyes he saw in the woods and the guardian angel that's been helping him. Could it have been her?

He let her go slowly, before continuing to walk. "So how do you know your way around Laquaderia so well?"

"Well I'm sort of a rebel," she chuckled in response.

"How so?"

"Well, my father is really protective and really old. Plus when he met Megahte, things became so different. So instead of spending a lot of time with him, or around the Covenant, I spend it alone so I can see the world. I guess that would be your answer."

"Our fathers knew each other?"

"They did, we're here," she finished as they neared a clearing that exposed a very small hut.

Alekos immediately exited the woods and began to walk towards the entrance, but before he could reach the door Azalea stepped in front of him. "I was just about to tell you---"

It was too late, the door opened and exposed the man inside.

"Azalea get inside."

It was the old man that Alekos saved from the cave. Azalea obediently trekked through the tense atmosphere before Alekos could open his mouth to say something, so he brushed past the old man after her. He was surprised to see stairs spiraling into the ground. There were no walls that separated the dirt, it was like going down into a mine. When he reached the bottom a den revealed itself that was much larger than the hut above.

"You brought me to him? *This* is your father?" Alekos stammered after catching up to Azalea.

"The old king is beyond your current reach, and what you need to hear he can't tell you. Only I can," the old man interrupted as he had followed them down.

"What I came here to do was warn the kingdom of a possible threat, I know exactly what I need to do now. I don't need your help, you didn't want to offer it earlier."

"I don't offer help, I offer knowledge. I can get your message to the kingdom, and you can be on your way."

Alekos gritted his teeth but then dropped his shoulders giving him a chance. The old man began to preach. "This might come as a surprise to you, but I'm almost a thousand years old."

"Nothing's a surprise anymore."

"Please don't interrupt," he instructed impatiently, before continuing. "I came across the Gorge with the first wave of life. I did not do this as a man though. I did it as a kitsune, or as many regards as a fox. It was thought that man and magic were completely separate, disregarding the centaurs that died out long ago. Until one day I turned into a man, unable to change back. I thought I was okay with it when I met a woman, and we fell in love. However, she aged much faster than I did. I made this home for her, because she accepted my unnatural self, and soon after she gave birth to our daughter Azalea. She was getting old, and weak, and didn't make it past the birth. She made me promise not to feel guilty because she knew I wouldn't be lonely."

"I'm so sorry to hear that," Alekos murmured as he looked to Azalea.

"It was soon after that I met Megahte that things began to change. More and more half breeds began to surface, and, in his discovery of his own form of magic, he placed himself in the middle of it. When he came to me and told me about your mother, and about his brother, and everything else he had done. I instructed him to build the Covenant and to keep my daughter out of it. Though it seems like she found it for herself," thc old man finished.

She looked down like a child faking shame for a guilty pleasure, before looking up to Alekos. He turned back to the old man, "So what is this knowledge that you have?"

"Well, besides more clarity of the situation, I believe you need information on what you're up against."

"I've seen the army, and tomorrow night the dinner bell rings."

"Let me be more specific. I believe you are still unaware of who leads this army, and what he's capable of. I doubt you had much time in your reunion he crashed."

"You sure do know a lot," Alekos stammered uncomfortably.

"It helps to have eyes and ears everywhere you have a concern with," the old man replied reassuringly.

"Then why didn't we get some kind of warning?" Alekos argued.

"As I said before, I want no part in this. Much less I want my daughter involved," he continued. "However, I will do what I can for you if it means her safety since I can't keep her under this roof. First, you need to be aware that he can do everything you can do and more. Most likely you will not win, but if you can outsmart him and buy time for reinforcements you might have a shot. Just make sure when Crewel arrives you have time to make up for your disagreement so that you may possibly be on a first-name basis. If you don't survive, we'll just have to see how history unfolds itself. And instead of saying anything else, I would take this knowledge and the time you can save to hurry back to your group before it disbands completely."

Chapter 12

"I have a feeling that your father knows a lot more than what he offered," Alekos began after a moment of silence.

It was evening now, and the sun was giving its final farewell before resting for the night. They had already made it most of the way back, and the tranquility between the two was caused by many factors. Alekos had pondered whether or not Azalea's choice to bring him to her father was worthwhile, but it was mostly due to all the stress that had accumulated and was ruminating throughout his head.

"I still feel like I'm walking into a mystery. I know everything about what's going on, except for nothing at all," he continued.

"You and me both," Azalea responded, "Megahte always kept me close, but never in his secrets, and my father has always told me he was dangerous. I never saw it, and I don't understand how they can be friends and when they never spoke to each other."

"It appears that we both have been kept in the dark," Alekos finished as the sun finally disappeared behind the horizon, leaving only the purple and pink sky in its absence.

"Yeah."

Azalea looked over to Alekos, her head sunk in guilt. She did know something. However, she decided to give him a bit of relief on his confusing journey by shedding light on one subject. "It was me in the woods following you around. Your father took many measures to make sure you made it to the Covenant. I would have brought you myself, but I was told not to interact with you."

"I had that thought, and thank you for your tears. I'm assuming you put that vial in Darc's bag, but why would he not want you to bring me if you had been following me from the beginning?"

"I don't know. Maybe he promised my father he wouldn't let me get in harm's way."

"Yeah, maybe," he added as they entered the clearing that they left the others in. Vrachos was still standing in the same spot by the campfire that had been kept alive; the others were not in sight.

Immediately, he felt his gut rise at the thought of his friends abandoning him. He couldn't hold the army off by himself, and even if he calls out his uncle there is no guarantee that he will honor it and keep everyone back. As they approached Vrachos, he shuddered and turned on a dime to see who was coming. It seems as though they had woke him with their footsteps.

Vrachos looked at them confused as if his vision was blurry due to crumbled earth crammed in the corners of his eyes. Suddenly rubble began to collapse from his body and a man stood in the place of the stone giant. He smiled and opened his mouth to speak, "Happy I am to see you. They left me for the fight."

"They left already?" Alekos stammered in disbelief. "How far are we behind?"

Vrachos tilted his head to the side and hummed as if thinking. He then put his hand to the ground, which opened obediently enough for his hand to slide in. He hummed once more as he stood, and responded, "They are stopped. Less than halfway there."

"Try to catch up with them Vrachos, tell them that we'll meet them at the entrance of Dead man's pass in the morning," Alekos ordered, "If I don't see you there, we'll wait. If you don't see us, make sure they wait."

Vrachos nodded and simultaneously he turned to run while rocks covered his body once more. He dove towards the ground, headfirst, and plunged straight in, leaving nothing behind but a circular patch of dirt where he landed in the grass.

Azalea looked up to see the astonished look on Alekos' face. She could tell he was fascinated with Vrachos' abilities.

"You know you'll be able to do the same once you master the medallion," Azalea whispered as she slid past him in the direction of the mountains.

Alekos swiftly kept pace with her, not wanting to waste time, and continued the conversation. "Do you think it will come to me, or is there a chance that I won't figure out how to work it in time?

"To be honest, I don't know. I do know that the medallion manipulates forces and can recreate the magic that you've encountered while wearing it."

"Darc told me that too when he was bringing me to the Covenant."

"Did he tell you that it awakens hidden powers from within humans?"

"Hidden powers?"

"The greatest weapon that humans have is their intellect. Somehow, the medallion can amp this trait to create telekinetic abilities. It also increases your reflexes. This is all I know about the medallion that you might not know yet."

"Well, I didn't know that. How did you?"

"I spent a lot of time with your father. He told me that before he encountered magic while wielding the medallion that he was able to do just that."

As she finished her sentence she swung her arm around towards Alekos' face. In a moment's notice, he had slipped beneath her arm and grabbed her fist before it finished its swing. "You see," she added with a cute laugh.

Alekos chuckled with her, he was impressed with himself as well. “So what do you do?” he asked as he let her go.

“I’m sorry,” she responded confused.

“Well everyone has some sort of magic here, and your father was a kitsune at one point. I know it’s a fox, but no one knew what they did.”

“That’s a surprise, considering it’s the animal for the kingdom’s banner I would think that was no mystery,” she joked.

“Very funny, you don’t have to show me. I just think it would be helpful for me to get exposed to a bit of magic beforehand, so I don’t walk into the fight empty-handed.”

She stopped and curled her face in thought as if debating on how to go about with this request. The next thing Alekos knew, he was holding her arm, with her fist in his hand, behind her back. “You see?” she added with a cute laugh.

He began to chuckle with her before letting her go immediately, his head felt dizzy. Déjà vu?

“Wow you picked that up quickly, I expected you to ask me what I do again.” She was smiling, and her eyes were gleaming with admiration.

“Did you –

“Time travel, yes,” she answered. “I can shift into my fox form on demand, unlike my father, and I can manipulate time and space and can even turn invisible. He shares that ability, but I lack his ability to age slowly due to my mother being human. My father can do much more than I. Including manifesting lightning and fire from his tails, and can even create illusions that people see as a reality. I hope to someday share these traits.”

“Wow, unbelievable. Your father is capable of all that?”

“Well he can’t turn into a fox anymore, so he can’t manifest anything from his tails. He had nine, and he fears because he can’t turn back that his time is running out.”

Alekos could see that this was a touchy subject for her, so he pulled her in close for a hug. She slid her hands beneath his arms and squeezed him towards her breasts. He could feel her heartbeat steadying itself on his chest.

He thought of what he could say, but before anything could come to his mind she let him go and continued.

“I may not be able to help you learn the medallion, but I

will help you with anything I can and I hope that we live to see the future in store for us."

He still seemed lost for words, as if her touch had completely dislocated his touch with reality. He just wanted to be back in her grasp. She slid her hands beneath his arms and squeezed him towards her breast. Again? He thought for sure she could read his mind, but before he could thank her she let him go and continued.

"I may not be able to help you learn the medallion, but I will help you with anything I can and—

"I hope we live to see the future in store for us," Alekos cut in, both guessing her sentence and flirting conspicuously.

She blushed immediately, as she had realized that he just accidentally time-traveled for another hug. "Was it hard to do that?" she interrogated, still blushing from his effort.

"To be honest, I didn't even know I did it. I was just thinking, and then suddenly déjà vu all over again," he answered innocently.

"You're sweet," she grinned, as her cheeks regained their natural appearance. She leaned up and kissed him on the cheek before continuing forward. "Make sure your head remains clear tomorrow night as well."

He smiled to himself, but he knew she was serious. He followed her in silence, his mind now grazing on the events that lie ahead of them. He thought of different ways he could use this newfound skill against his opponent, but every way led to a gamble with his life in order to be one step ahead.

Suddenly he realized that that's not the only ability he's seen, and just as he thought of it his point of view began to rise. He looked at his hands to see the ground tumbling upwards onto his body turning him into a stone giant. As his hands formed their new shape, finalizing the transformation, he looked up to see Azalea staring right at him.

"This is awesome," he bellowed, causing the enchanted birds sleeping in the trees around them to take flight. He began to chuckle only to realize that Azalea was about to lose her balance. Immediately he shed the stones, as he looked at her apologetically.

She shook her head while smiling, amused with his

childish behavior. “Anything else you’d like to try?” she joked sarcastically.

With that statement, another thing occurred to him. Darc could teleport. “Actually, there is.”

She shook her head once more, still smiling. However, he remained in place with nothing but a confused look on his face.

“I don’t think it’s working,” he sighed perplexed and disappointed. She asked him something, but he was too deep in thought to know that she was trying to help. What was it that his father told him? Every shadow was like a window to him.

“Who are you trying to copy?” she said again, finally breaking through his thoughts.

However, instead of replying he looked around, noticing that they were covered in darkness. Window? The next thing he knew he was falling but he never hit the ground. All he could see around him was darkness, and he couldn’t move.

“Alekos? Alekos!” He could hear Azalea screaming from above, but when he looked up he couldn’t see her. Only the pitch-black void that he was trapped in.

“Azalea!” he cried up, realizing he messed up something. However, she continued to call for him as if she never heard him.

Suddenly another noise caught his attention. It sounded like a mixture between a woman moaning in pain and the wind whistling through the trees. He looked about, seeing nothing of course, before a cold gust swept past him and its icy grip twirled him around.

He could feel the cold digging through his pores, stretching around his tendons and tightening them. His ribs began to suck in as he lost his breath as if something was sucking it out of him. His heart began to race as it dove into his stomach. This couldn’t be it.

He couldn’t see anything, but he knew his vision was fading. He could feel his conscious slipping, and he tried to think but only images were coming through. His life was flashing before his eyes, and then, in an instant, he knew what to do. The next thing he knew, he could see a tattered cloth-covered phantom encircling his body like a snake. Its teeth were dug into his neck.

It didn’t matter. Despite realizing that Darc’s eyes

captured darkness instead of light, he couldn't break free from the grasp. Once more, through his blood pounding eardrums, he heard Azalea faintly crying out his name. He looked up to see that he was underneath her as if she were floating on the surface of the water that was drowning him. He was so far away though, and he couldn't break free. The grip was so tight he couldn't call up to her either. All he could think of was how stupid he was for messing around with magic, and how he wished he could be next to her.

Suddenly his body slipped from the creature, zooming towards Azalea, but it wasn't giving up easily and before he completely broke free from its grip he skidded to a halt. He looked down to see the beast holding his ankles tight with its tail, and pulling against the force that was trying to rescue him. He heard it make its noise once more, and it was answered by others in different directions.

He gazed around to see more phantoms slivering through the darkness towards him in all directions. He looked up once more at Azalea and closed his eyes, this was it. He wasn't going to escape this time. Then he realized the noises stopped, and he was warming up. He opened his eyes to see Azalea smiling at him.

"Anything else you'd like to try?" she joked sarcastically, before seeing his face. He was hollow even though his vitals had returned to normal. The shock mixed with his gratitude for what she had done froze him in place. "Is everything okay?" she questioned, her face curled with worry.

He finally broke free from his trance and took a deep breath. "Uh... yeah, and no, there's nothing else I'd like to try," he answered with a fake chuckle. She studied him unconvinced, but shrugged it off and motioned him to keep walking not wanting to waste time. He nodded and followed.

He couldn't help but appreciate her for not delving into what had happened. It was almost as she didn't know that anything did happen. Either way, he was happy to be safe, and happy to be walking with her once again.

Chapter 13

By the time they made it to the mountains, Alekos had done gotten over his close encounter with death. It seemed to be almost second nature to him to have his life at risk. The night was solemn as it usually was in the wilderness. They had gathered fluorescent mushrooms along the way to create a light stack. They couldn't go into the pass until Vrachos arrived, and creating a fire could draw unwanted attention from the mountains.

Alekos practiced a few of his newfound skills by creating a bench from the ground. It wasn't impressive, and Azalea had an amusing time watching him trials. However, he eventually made one quite suitable and they sat and waited, in silence for a while.

Light was finally peaking its orange hue, and the mushrooms were transcending from their baby blue light to a mellow turquoise when the silence when broken. It was Azalea who spoke first.

"You know I didn't realize that your eyes change colors, I've never seen anyone whose eyes do that."

He chuckled but didn't say anything at first. When he was young people thought he was just as weird as Elrin for the same reason.

"What are you thinking about?" She questioned, almost worried-like.

He looked up to her, her eyes were reflecting in the mushroom light; the color was a perfect match. He smiled and opened his mouth to speak before a sound disturbed the serenity and snatched his attention. Never could he just pretend like life was normal. They spun around towards the growing noise that now vibrated the ground beneath them and the mountains. Suddenly, the ground began to crumble and light fiercely exploded from the crevices as the earth slowly fell. Alekos quickly hopped to his feet in defense.

"Stay back!" He stammered at Azalea.

As dust consumed the blinding light, and the shaking concluded, figures began to rise from the ground. The shape of the largest shadow gave away the identity of the hostiles. It didn't take long for his chest to stop pounding, and Alekos chuckled as he relaxed and approached the group.

It was Vrachos and the ones that decided to come. As the dust cleared it became obvious that the blinding light was Pyrus' head engulfed like a torch, which too began to simmer. Four others stood with them, a shy number compared to the number that the covenant used to boast. Darc, Xarth and two others he wasn't completely familiar with, though of course he had seen them.

"We don't have many fighters as you can see, but I'll admit I'm glad you're here," Darc started, "This is Dmitri and Lakyn. Dmitri and Lakyn are responsible for the ecosystem of the covenant, with Dmitri controlling earthly life and Lakyn with water in respect. Dmitri's sister, Vyne, is with the rest, and will do her best in keeping them hidden."

"Well I won't doubt that each of you has something to bring, but we're completely outnumbered, possibly outmatched," Alekos pointed out.

"So what's the plan," Darc said as the group came together.

"I can get us in," Azalea softly interrupted.

Everyone looked amongst each other, obviously unaware of her skills as Alekos has been, but Alekos nodded and continued.

"The portal seemed to be generating in the middle of the Colosseum so I assume that's where we'll find my uncle waiting, and that's where we need to focus the battle. If we split up we'll be outnumbered, and no one can protect the other. So we stay together. I only got a glimpse from far off, so there's no telling how much danger we're walking into. There's not much time, so let's get going." Alekos concluded, ending their conversation.

Ready to relinquish their life for the sake of the world, they set out in the direction of Dead Man's Gorge through the tunnel that Vrachos had started. It was faster this way, and safer for the Gorge was full of death. It wasn't long before they were there as they sped along on a slab of stone as the earth opened and closed around them in the direction they had to go. As it stopped the earth dissolved above them as they rose to the surface and Pyrus once again put out his head.

Alekos then turned to look beyond them. There it was. The great structure from his vision. Lightning scratched the sky, lighting the peninsula, and thunder billowed around them, echoing between the walls of the ravine behind them.

They all stared in awe until a purple light appeared above the colosseum followed by another burst of lightning.

"The realms are tying," Azalea shouted aloud as the wind began to pick up deafening the air, "We need to go now!"

They all started towards the entrance of the structure, crossing the strip of land that bridged the peninsula to the lands. However, every step they took, the tear between the realms grew larger.

They flooded into the ruins and quickly made their way to the court in the middle of the colosseum.

"Can you get us in," Alekos asked Azalea catching his breath, but before she could reply a surge of electricity zapped from inside the void. They looked as something poked its head out from the darkness above. Then another appeared, and another.

"Oh shit," Alekos burst as he realized what it was, "Get ready!"

The beast turned his head towards Alekos, hearing him, and let out a roar that shook the ruins. Then suddenly it leaped from the hole, its wings outstretched. It could fly.

Then one by one more flying beast began to emerging and soaring from the void. They all were focused on the group and dived down to attack. The battle had begun.

Xarth was the first to act, casting a bolt of lightning from his hand to the first beast that attacked. It fell and smacked into the earth violently and immediately the rest retaliated to seek vengeance.

Vrachos grew and started to swat at the monsters. His massive size quickly took them down in a single blow. They were relentless though. Continuously the beast swarmed down, as the group got pushed apart. Pyrus was defending Azalea with Dmitri

Dmitri created vines that snatched the beasts from the air and anchored them to the ground as Pyrus lit them on fire. Then Alekos realized he was doing nothing, but what could he do. Then suddenly the ground shook as the large beast landed in front of them.

Everyone was too busy to notice though. Darc was in the air, appearing from the underbelly of one beast to the next, disemboweling them. Xarth was shocking one after another as they flooded out the void, and Lakyn was condensing shards of ice from the storm above and impaling as many as he could. As each one hit the ground, the earth shuddered in pain leaving everyone incognizant of the straggler.

Alekos charged towards the beast, unwilling to let it catch them off guard but was quickly swatted aside as Vrachos charged and hoisted the beast up, grabbing it around its necks.

The heads twisted and snapped at his rock body to no avail until one dragon head opened its mouth and flames spewed out slowly consuming his body. Vrachos let out a roar as he charged it backward smacking it into a wall, and, as it collapsed to the ground, proceeded in wailing down at the heads.

Alekos got to his feet and drew his sword just as he was snatched off the ground.

“Ahhh,” he cried out as the claws from the beast dug into his shoulders. He looked down to see the colosseum shrinking beneath him, and the battle raging below.

He grabbed at the leg of what looked like a hippogryph with a bull's head instead of an eagle's. Then suddenly the pain in his shoulder stretched down his arm and chest. He looked at his arm to see scales growing on his skin, and no blood coming from his shirt. He swung his sword up and like a blade through water it sliced clean through the leg holding him.

He fell as the pained stretched across his body, and then he heard a voice. It was familiar.

"Stop fighting the pain, it's who you are," said the feminine voice. It was his mother's voice.

Then he felt his bones popping again in his back, and once more he screamed out as he plummeted towards the ground. He looked at his now scaly hands that were growing talon-like claws and then closed his eyes as he neared the ground.

Anticipating the imminent impact he closed his eyes and took a deep breath. The next moment he collided with the surface, he felt the earth crush beneath him as he struck the ground, creating a sound wave that shook the colosseum.

Ringing reverberated inside Alekos' head as he realized he wasn't dead, he shook his head as he lifted his chest off the ground and looked around. Everyone was fighting. Vrachos was still on the beast, which now lay dead crushed beneath him, but was now focused on another pair that swatted at him from above.

Alekos fell back down as his back arched up, searing in pain. His shirt could be heard ripping as something burst through it and Alekos let out another cry. Then another landed in front of him that drew his attention.

He looked up to see a dragon hunched over, snarling through its teeth. Hot steam escaped it's nostrils as it grunted.

Alekos picked up his sword and pushed himself to his feet, just as the beast started to charge. It opened its mouth and fire filled the air between them, and Alekos quickly dived to the side. He turned back to see that he had traveled thirty feet as he rolled back onto his feet.

That's when he realized what was on his back. He straightened his posture as the wind gusted ever more comfortably than before. There were wings back there. The dragon turned back facing Alekos and leaped towards him, spreading its wings. In a split second, Alekos soared over it slicing a wing off.

As he landed on the ground he turned to see the wounded beast picking itself up, obviously pissed off. *I could get used to this*, he chuckled inside. Again, the two charged at each other and Alekos swung once more, but missed as the dragon jumped up onto its back feet.

It came down to stomp on Alekos, who raised his hand to stop it and suddenly a pulse of energy expelled itself from his hand and sent the dragon flying back. It rolled backward before catching its ground, only giving Alekos a short moment to enjoy his newfound powers.

The beast went to charge again, but suddenly a boulder disintegrated itself as it crushed again the side of the dragon, sending its corpse rolling to the side.

Then another bolt of lightning went off as the last beast fell dead from the void. The battle had ended. Alekos caught his breath and turned to see everyone was alive.

Everyone turned to look at Alekos and drew back. He resembled a man but looked like a dragon, and his eyes burned bright through the night. Darc suddenly appeared in front of him with a blade to his throat.

"It's me," Alekos burst when he realized that Darc thought he was a beast.

"Oh shit," Darc exclaimed as he let him go, "You're lucky those scales are strong, I tried to slice you a new mouth, haha. How did you transform like that?"

Alekos stared blankly back. "I don't know," he murmured as his body slowly returned to normal. "Could my father not?"

"We have to keep going," Azalea interrupted as she looked up at the still-growing void, "We won't have long once we're on the other side to stop them before they'll be able to crossover."

"Everyone, gather around me," she demanded as she stood under the portal. After they were in a close huddle she turned to Xarth, "Strike it. "

He raised his hand obediently and everything began to spin violently and suddenly halted making them all nearly nauseous. However, an awful clatter quickly brought them to senses, and they realized everything around them had changed.

The night sky was covered in dark clouds, which reflected the dancing fires that burned outside the colosseum. The air shook from the monstrous raucous, and the group immediately tensed. "The portal will freeze over temporarily due to our passage through, they will know we're here because of this," Azalea started, "We need to get ready."

As soon as she said that, a voice echoed across the stadium. "You!?"

Everyone turned to look at the voice. It came from the entrance of the arena. It was a man. He raised a hand and suddenly the beasts flooded over the high walls into the balconies and stands surrounding them.

They quickly raised their guard and huddled closer and closer as the horde engulfed their surroundings, consuming every bit of room to move and think. Within seconds they were encircled, leaving only a hallway between them and the man.

As he loomed closer revealing the wretched details of his old, despicable face, the swarm closed in. He was a man etched with death and destruction, and as he approached his lips curved revealing his sly and maniacal heart. He was bathing happily in the moment.

Alekos immediately stepped in front of his group.

"Oh, he's good. He's really good," Kojax laughed as he walked closer and the army swallowed the area around them. They huddled closer, but Alekos stepped once more towards the man.

"That's right, I'm here to finish this!" Alekos roared to the man, who just chuckled. .

"Finish what exactly, what did Megahte tell you," Kojax mocked pitifully, then smiled. "This will be fun."

Alekos had heard enough, he pulled his sword out and almost instinctively his body armored up. "I know everything I need to know. Let's settle this, you and me only. The winner goes through the hole." The boiling anger that swelled inside him was quickly overpowering his patience.

Kojax lips once more sharply curved a wicked grin, "Too easy."

The next moment a blade was to Alekos' throat, and a hand fiercely yanked his hair back. "Are you ready to die over a lie?" Kojax hissed into his ears, then spun him around as everyone jerked. "I will have no resistance!" His roar echoed and rumbled amongst the grim storm above.

Alekos fought the tears that swelled as a stone of disappointment anchored his stomach to a bottomless pit. He ferociously darted his gaze to everyone, who's hard stare exemplified their fear, and anger began to boil as he mulled over all the people who's been led to their death in the pursuit of his protection and welfare.

"You could never win!" Kojax roared snapping Alekos back to reality. "I've had fifteen years to build my army and hone my skills. Megahte mobilized vagrants, and gave his job to a child! You have no cause to join besides deception."

"No cause? You sent men for me and mother just in case my father beat you, and all for what? Because he didn't need you anymore to protect him. The irony is the one destined to stop you turned out to be an orphan who never needed anyone neither. You're a child throwing a tantrum."

Alekos could feel the blade creeping into his throat, breaking through the scales that formed in defense, then suddenly it was removed. The grip on his hair tightened, then he was thrown to the ground. He pushed himself to his feet and picked his sword up, then spun around and jabbed it towards Kojax.

It drove into his stomach, and Alekos looked into what looked like eyes of sorrow before his sword grew stiff and the body turned to stone. Suddenly an elbow met the side of his face, and his vision blacked out as he fell to his knees. With double vision, he looked up anticipating another attack, but it was apparent Kojax wasn't trying to kill him.

He crept over to Alekos, grabbing the trapped sword as the stone body crumbled. "You have been manipulated far worse than I. You know nothing, and have more reason to hate everyone around you than I. Especially Megahte above all others. So let me open your eyes, and maybe you'll learn you have no cause to fight for."

Suddenly a flame engulfed Kojax's body, as Pyrus decided to take advantage of Alekos' freedom. Kojax turned in the fire, growing as scales ruptured from his skin, and the next moment Pyrus was in his grip. Pyrus exploded into flames as he tried to fight Kojax off, but as Kojax tightened his grip on Pyrus' throat the flames, too, suffocated and simmered down to steam. Before anyone could react, fire began to spew from Pyrus' eyes as he screamed frantically, Kojax' silver medallion was consuming the magic from his soul.

"What did I say about resistance!" He screamed as Pyrus squirmed and kicked fruitlessly.

"You're killing him!" Alekos cried out as he bounced to his feet. But a wave of energy knocked him to his back and he looked up to see Pyrus' pale lifeless body cripple onto the ground as Kojax let him go. Without notice, Vrachos let out a rattling siren and pounded the ground. Everywhere around them, the ground began to flip crushing the surrounding army and a club was in his hand. Then instantly it stopped as Vrachos froze like a statue, both arms over his head with the club, as his segments solidified.

"Enough!" fumed Kojax, "I've killed every one of you before! I can do everything you can do!"

No one wanted to listen, but no one wanted to get the rest killed either, as painful as it was. "Does anyone want to know the truth?" Kojax asked as he went back to his despicable smile. "The truth that Megahte isn't who I know he's claiming to be." He turned to Alekos, who was distraught in the emotional turmoil that just flared.

"Look at me! Do you not see the truth! We have the same scales, the same sword, and the same eyes! While I sat in a world that wasn't real, with people that weren't real, you were living a life that wasn't real. Being fed an illusion that wasn't real, but it's time to wake up. Megahte isn't your father, and I sent no one to kill you until the realms began to tie just this week. The fifteen years I spent was not from the moment the fight ended between him and me, but the fifteen years that led up to it. You and I are one and the same. Who else has eyes that change colors?"

"Are you insane!?" Alekos cried in disbelief, as he faced his group that was holding onto Pyrus' body.

Kojax met his gaze, "You should be happy that he lived that long. In my past, Pyrus was buried alive as an infant because he was an uncontrollable disaster. I'm not asking you to believe me, I'm telling you; this is the truth. Megahte targeted every single one of you because he knew you existed and knew where to find you. Anyone who died was just a pawn to begin with. He was never a father, only a thief and a liar. Like I said. Look at me!"

As he finished his eyes changed from their burning amber to a crisp emerald, and Alekos' felt his heart sink. *It couldn't be true? Could it?* He spent his whole life avoiding eye contact because the one thing he knew was that his eyes changed colors. That was his birthmark. Suddenly his body yanked upwards and Kojax clenched hold of his tunic. The burning torches of his army waved in the reflection of his scales. He turned his gaze up and continued to speak.

"The time is almost here!" He shouted as the void above began to crack through the ice and swell towards the arena. "Do you want to want to go back to your world with your friends and make a world of half breeds with me, or do you want to die with them! The choice is yours."

As he finished he let Alekos go, who stumbled back completely overwhelmed.

Chapter 14

Within moments the colosseum was consumed by the void, and a decision had to be made. Impatiently, Kojax seized Dmitri by the shoulder and gouged his talons into his shoulder, engulfing them in flames.

"Well?" He demanded.

"Okay! Okay, you win..." Alekos uttered, giving up.

Almost immediately he let him go, a twisted, withered stump was what remained of his shoulder as he collapsed faintly to his knees.

"Well don't act so glum about it then, you all should be ecstatic! I'm making this whole world a home for you guys," he simpered with a swing of his arm, and suddenly the group was each picked up by his spherical creations. "Them I just don't quite trust yet. I'm sure you can understand."

Alekos remorsefully stared at his helpless comrades. Darc was surrounded by light; Lakyn was in a shell of earth; Dmitri was encased in stone, as was Xarth before it burst into flames as turned into glass. Despite their efforts, they were truly disabled.

Then he realized Azalea wasn't among them.

"You can't capture a kitsune," Kojax interrupted, clearly reading Alekos' expression change. "Deceitful little devils, take my word for it."

He passed Alekos without hesitation and began to stride towards the entranceway. Once more his army parted for him, as he led the defeated group out the colosseum. Alekos reluctantly followed. As they stepped beyond the walls of the structure the burning sky melted into pouring rain. As his clothes drenched, a weight swelled inside of him. He truly was a pawn, and he hated how much he agreed with Kojax. His dwelling was short-lived as Kojax hollered in exhilaration.

"Look at all the precious water!" He exclaimed, "I'd say pinch me, but I'd kill you if I woke up."

He continued to laugh as he turned for the mainland. Simultaneously, a rumble erupted as his horde bled from the colosseum. The walk was tedious, as Dead Man's Gorge wasn't a straight path. It incorporated a series of steep climbs and narrow ridges. Despite the rain running off the mountaintop, only Alekos seemed to struggle as the massive army swept over the surrounding mountains like a blanket being pulled.

He watched as all the nightmares of the mountains were slaughtered mercilessly as they crept from their holes. The giant spiders, the spiked wyverns, and the massive man-like lycanthropes all fell powerlessly to the legion. Once more he felt both pity, for the lack of humanity, and a strange feeling of security. Was Kojax a bad man, or does he truly care for peace and equality between the mundane and the mystical? Was this brutality, or was this preservation of the world beyond the mountains?

"Do you know why we deserve this?" Kojax hollered to Alekos who was scrambling behind. "Because the world kept both you and me from knowing we were half breeds."

Alekos slipped but quickly was pressed onto his feet by a wave of energy. He looked up to see Kojax reaching his hand out to help him up. He was no longer covered in scales. "You heard me correctly," he teased, as he pulled him up. "But here is the kicker; we're the first to be naturally born from human parents. I didn't know this at first until Mother told me. The same day, the woman I loved chose another. The next day, Megahte was wielding what he kept me from knowing. He took everything from me, even the stone that forged our medallions."

For the first time, clarity was a friend. Everything started to make sense, and everything he's experienced was due to Megahte being ill-prepared for the repercussions of his actions. Though he couldn't help but jest that this all began with a rock. Suddenly, everyone halted as they reached the final descent. Alekos caught up to notice the massive army that littered the ground and forest below. It was Crewel's army; the old man had delivered the message. Yet Alekos doubted their success, let alone their survival.

"Let me ask you something," Alekos finally spoke, alarming Kojax.

"At last you're awake!" He cheered.

"You made monsters from people, I've seen it," Alekos continued. "Let me go down and convince them to stand down. Even if you do it again they keep their lives."

"And let you fight for them, I don't think so!" Kojax argued as he raised his hand to signal.

"Please, take the medallion," Alekos pleaded, halting the command, "I just don't want any more people to die because of me. They're here and ready to fight because of me."

Kojax tightened his jaw, as he gritted his teeth, before letting out a sigh. "Fine. You have two minutes."

Obediently, he surrendered his medallion and began the descent. His mind was ruminating too much too care, pondering what he could say to save everyone's lives. As he neared the sloping plain, which descended towards the magnificent display of devotion below, a figure came from within the midst of the mass. It was Crewel.

"I thought you were supposed to hold them off," he scorned as they neared each other.

"We tried," Alekos retorted.

"No, we wouldn't be talking if you tried," Crewel spat back.

"Listen to me. We can't defeat him, but we can still survive. No one has to die," Alekos argued, as the tension rose.

"You truly are a traitorous bastard," Crewel retaliated as

he withdrew his sword, which ensued a deafening raucous on both sides.

Instinctively, Alekos withdrew his. "You truly are a self-centered prick."

Crewel immediately changed his expression and withdrew his demeanor, but then drew up once again. "Where did you get that sword?!"

Alekos withdrew himself, perplexed, but Crewel demanded an answer. As the blade reached his throat, Alekos blurted his response. "You wouldn't care! I took it from a dead man who killed my mother and took it from her blood-stained hands!"

Suddenly, Crewel dropped his sword and began stepping back as if pierced in the heart. Everything became still, and the ambiance hushed. Tears swelled in corner of Crewel's eyes. "It can't be. Just couldn't be.."

"What?"

He was in shock, but he came forward, alarming Alekos, and stopped just short. He stared hard into Alekos' eyes, just briefly, before pulling him in and embracing him.

"Brother," Crewel sighed genuinely, as he clutched tighter, but Alekos briskly pushed away.

"No one could possibly have known that. It has to be you," Crewel asserted.

Again, turmoil trembled throughout Alekos as he tried to keep his bearings. Everything was abruptly spinning and tying together, and the enlightenment was near nauseating. Before he could react or respond, the tranquility was broken by a roar from behind. He snatched his head back to see Kojax's swarm cascading towards them. It was too late. He turned back, Crewel had already armed himself. They gazed once more at each other, and it was apparent what they had to do.

Crewel raised his arm and brought his blade down, commanding his army to charge. Alekos turned to run but was yanked back. "I'm not losing you again. Every woman and child is at the castle, it's your turn to keep them safe."

With that, Crewel turned and began to charge as Alekos stood frozen as Crewel had earlier. The ground began to tremble as each knight escalated the ascent, rushing past Alekos and towards their fate. In moments, he was standing alone in a cloud of dust with nothing but the loud yells ahead to keep him company.

Just before the clash, a petrifying noise cracked the heavens, and an ominous shadow swooped overhead. The winged creature plummeted towards the soldiers, and, with a piercing hiss, began to spew fire, catching them ablaze. As they screamed, the army of monsters submerged into the fiery lake and slaughtered them as they scattered in disarray.

"Nooo!" Alekos cried, as the barbaric slaughter burned and stained his memory. He turned his head away and closed his eyes, begging that he would wake, but fell to his knees as the screams began to drown him in anguish.

Everyone's life was truly ending, and it was entirely his fault. Both he and his doppelganger were to blame. His vision was overwhelmed in tears, but he didn't wipe them or fight them. All the pain was just unleashing inside him, and he didn't know what to do. If only he had seized an opportunity sooner, or had more patience. Maybe he could have stopped Kojax in the beginning.

Suddenly, he was jerked up by his nape. "Your time was up," Kojax croaked, as he forced Alekos to stand. "We don't need this resistance in our new world. Isn't it just beautiful?" It was over. The savages were walking around finishing off those still breathing, while many more came over the ridge. "Our medallions function entirely two different ways, and together we would rule as gods. With you harvesting magic, and me manipulating it, we could live forever. Making life how we please."

He released Alekos and pulled out the medallion. "Do you stand with me or not?"

Alekos was listening though. His mind had done escaped him. He turned around, his face completely apathetic. He was only thinking of the woman and children hidden in the forest and the castle. On his waist, a bag sat open, and his fist was clenched. He looked up to Kojax and smiled. "No," he laughed. "I'm just not feeling it." Kojax grew stern before seeing a marble appear in Alekos' fingers.

"Ever wonder what it's like when you die?"

He squeezed it, imagining an explosion that would cover the mountains, and...

Everything went white and his ears were ringing violently. He tried to cover his ears, but nothing changed. He felt nothing, not even his arms moving. He tried to scream, but nothing came out and the ringing began to grow until it was just a faint hum. The next moment, colors began to swirl around him, and he too felt a spinning motion despite still not seeing his body amongst the swirl of returning colors. Then suddenly he found himself floating, intangible and obscured from his senses, inside the old man's home. Azalea was there, and so was he, but he was completely different.

Azalea sat in the opposite room, while the old man hovered over the short-haired, brute Alekos. He had gashed wounds all over his body, and a fatal one at the throat. The old man pulled out a vile and began pouring its contents over the wounds, which retaliated with hissing and smoke. In seconds, the wounds vanished leaving not a trace behind. The man then wrung a cloth from a bucket and began to clean the crimson stains that remained. Without notice, the Alekos sprang up screaming and the man pressed him back down.

"You're quite alright. I'm sure you had quite the scare. Take it easy, it's going to be alright," the old man reassured him. Heavy of breath, the Alekos slowly obeyed as he lay back down. As his breathing regulated, the man returned to cleaning the blood.

"Do you remember anything about what happened?"

The Alekos looked over to the man and paused before reaching up quickly for his neck.

"It was a dream, but it's fixed up. You can talk," the old man continued. "Do you remember who did that to you? How they did it?"

The Alekos cleared his throat then began slowly. "A man who could move through the shadows. A nightmare."

"You are a curious one, that's why I saved you. There is something inside you that is meant for something bigger than you know. What you met was the beginning of a new dawn; a new species. Magic is crossing paths with humans, and you just crossed paths with one of them. Quite savage I'd admit, but I wouldn't say he's very welcomed anywhere."

"I need to get back to my brother, he needs to know about this," the Alekos uttered as he tried to get up from the bed.

"Oh no you don't," the old man argued as he pressed him back down.

"Do you know who I am?" the Alekos asserted as he pressed himself back up.

"I do," the man answered, "You are the second son of the great king. Your name is Kojax Sacahte, and your brother is Crewel Mega. You are known as the Sacamega brothers because you're never apart. Your brother goes by Megahte because he doesn't like his name. There is nothing I don't know. So trust me when I tell you to stay."

"What do you want?" Kojax demanded.

"I want you to discover your path," the old man answered as he pulled out a stone. "I want you to rest. When you wake up, take this stone, to your brother if you must, and chase the magic. As I said, it's a new dawn, and we'll need a proper leader."

"A rock. You want me to take a rock."

"I want you to take the Stone of Origenesis , and make the right choice."

Suddenly, the scene began to grow distant and Alekos found himself flying through the ground above the hermitage. Torches were lit in the distance, and as they neared it became clear that it was a slimmer, fitter Crewel and Kojax. It was clear that time had passed since the last scene.

"As I said, this is where I woke up after being attacked by the so-called fictitious man," Kojax could be heard insisting as they approached.

"I don't care if this old man exists, I'm going to end this nonsense. He's a lonely old man playing with your mind. Do you really believe you were killed and then brought back to life completely unscathed by an old man?" Megahte contented. "It's not possible."

"If I'm making it up, why not let me keep the rock and entertain my imagination?"

"You're not seeing this from a clear perspective. You

shouldn't feed his insanity."

"Hey! Boys! Can you keep it down, my dad is trying to sleep." interrupted a familiar female voice. Both guys turned to look at Azalea, and they both paused as their fires danced across her skin. Megahte shook his head loose first.

"I apologize completely, ma'am. Please accept my appreciation for taking care of my brother, but, if you could return this to your father for me," he responded shyly as he up his hand over hers. However, nothing fell from his hand. "You have a good night now."

He turned back towards Kojax, and that's when everything began to spin and once more Alekos was somewhere new. It appeared as though he was in the castle, but he didn't recognize the room. Books were scattered everywhere, some were ripped and others were open on top of each other. Vials of chemicals were assorted on a table in front of Megahte, who was working vigorously with couplings for a golden chain. The door busted open, and light flooded the room, causing Megahte to slam his hands onto the table.

"What is it!?" Megahte scolded the intruder.

"Your brother is trying to go out on a mission with us."

"Well tell him to meet me in the courtyard if he's bored. I'll be there at sunset to test his footwork. Whatever you do, you don't let him go on those runs with you."

"Yes, sir."

As the man turned away Alekos turned to see a map of their world marked in different locations, but then began flying towards the light of the closing door. Before he collided, though, he found himself slowly turning back around. Everything in the room had been trashed. Kojax was standing in the middle of the room, panting. As Alekos hovered closer, he could see, in Kojax's hands, half the stone and parchments of work that Megahte had completed. As he turned his eyes were glowing orange. The orange glow grew until Alekos found himself falling from the sky with the first drops of rain, and, as he peered down, he once again found himself plummeting to the colosseum.

The storm had grown powerful, by the time he halted, and Alekos found himself in a raging battle between the Sacamega brothers. They were moving so fast, conducting so much, Alekos could hardly keep track of the fight. However, it was clear that Megahte was losing. Every time he would dart, or disappear, Kojax would see through and catch him in the landing. Alekos wondered why he didn't just leave entirely, but it soon became apparent that he was trying to talk to Kojax; trying his best to get through to him.

"The world wasn't ready, you weren't ready," Megahte cried as they collided into a stalemate.

"Yet you were? That wasn't your decision to make!"

Kojax solidified the swords together with stone then used them to bash Megahte's shield from his hand. Once unarmed, the stone crumbled from the swords sending Megahte's to the ground. With a quick motion, Kojax swung his blade backing Megahte to a wall. "You don't deserve to be a king. Once father sees how I can control this new age, and learns how you died trying to hide them from the world, he'll hand me the crown. Goodbye brother!"

He pulled his arm back before lunging forward, Megahte raised his arms in defense, and then suddenly Kojax was no longer beside him. Megahte collapsed backward into the wall and reached up to his chest, which was now painted in blood. He tried to breathe, but the pain was sharp. He leaned forward and reached for his sword. As his hand clenched the tip, it burst into flames, and he pulled it towards his chest. He cried as he cauterized the wound on his chest, and then vanished.

Fog rolled past Alekos' vision, and, as it dissipated, he could make out Megahte inching his way through the forest, which was now covered in the night's dark blanket. In the distance, there was a familiar hermitage. As he neared, he let out a yawp which resulted in a gust of wind and a low rumble in the sky. He continued to walk and he stopped as he reached the door.

"I'm sorry it came to this. Goodbye, brother."

He kicked open the door, coinciding with a crash of lightning, and a woman could be seen inside. She was shaking, both hands clenched tight to a sword. Alekos' heart sunk. It was his mother. He tried to scream, but, again, no noise came out. Megahte withdrew a dagger and the next moment he was behind her, gripping her around the nape. The knife was pressed to her throat.

"Hello Mother," he hissed as he dragged the blade across

her neck.

He let her go and she fell to her knees, trying to hold back the waterfall that began to expel. He picked up the sword she dropped and placed it into his empty sheath then turned towards the door. Alekos tried to close his eyes, and was surprised when his vision blacked out. However, he realized, soon after, that he was transitioning once more. He found himself by a bridge, and a very young woman was tossing a piece of meat into the water. He watched as the beta angels tore up the meat, and then realized the lady wasn't paying attention to the fish anymore. She had noticed something.

He hovered over her as she made her way off the bridge and crept closer to the bank. Then suddenly she ran through the water, hopping hysterically as the betas tore up the meat nearby. She was incredibly daring. It wasn't until his vision caught up to her that he noticed what she had seen. It was a little boy. It was him. She reached down and took off the royal patch on his tunic.

Then everything went black. He quickly realized that he could smell, and the aroma was familiar. He opened his eyes, blinking several times, before realizing he was in the old man's house. He rose up slowly and looked around. Two shadows could be seen heard softly discussing something inaudible from a room opposite of him. He looked around and quickly noticed that he was lying exactly where Kojax had been.

He reached for his ripped and bloody shirt on the floor, but then stopped with his arm outstretched. It was bigger. He quickly reached up to his head, and, sure enough, it was shaggy. *What the hell is going on?* He went to stand, but, without notice, the two were standing before him. It was Azalea and her dad.

"I hope one of you is about to tell me what's going on," Alekos muttered.

"You have been given the privilege to see your life unfold," the old man started. "It may have been an illusion, but you lived that reality. Again, I must tell you to take this stone. The choice you make is entirely up to you… Kojax."

He held out his hand, and in his palm was the stone of Origenesis .

www.ingramcontent.com/pod-product-compliance
Lightning Source LLC
Chambersburg PA
CBHW070626310726
48982CB00001B/175

* 9 7 8 0 5 7 8 5 9 9 3 6 6 *